Sunshine through the Rain

C.A. COLLINS

First Edition

PAGE PUBLISHING, INC.
New York, NY

First originally published by Page Publishing, Inc. 2018

ISBN 978-1-64424-713-6 (Paperback)
ISBN 978-1-64424-714-3 (Digital)

Printed in the United States of America

For Mike – you make crazy sane.

Preface

Life can break you six ways to Sunday – if you let it. I grew up in the South, in the tough section of the south where fists fly, and the word nigger is used in everyday conversation. Black people are killed, and their deaths are never avenged, women are raped, and no one is punished. "She was wearing a short skirt. She asked for it." It is a hot, humid, scary place where tempers flare quickly and often. Yet, there are also things in the South that don't exist anywhere else. The smell of magnolia and jasmine. Those Williams boys – Hank and Tennessee. SEC football – Geaux Tigers! Coonhounds lazily resting under front porch swings. Chicken and Dumplings, fried chicken, fresh tomatoes off the vine. It is easy to remember the bad but take a beat and think about the good. Wade through the creek, make a mud pie, chase tadpoles – immerse yourself in the gentile breeze and the stories of the characters in this book. I hope you will find something of yourself in each of the people you read about and come to feel an affinity for them. Thank you, Dear Reader, for taking the time to walk down this winding, dirt road with me. I think you will be better for it.

Acknowledgements

Thank you to my father Grady Collins for teaching me a turn of phrase and a love of stories told on dusky evenings. Thank you to my other mother Kathy for your love and friendship. Thank you to my children Scott, Lindsey, Matt, and Mark for your unconditional support and your ability to always make me laugh. For my grandchildren, Riley and Zayne – you are my Sunshine – my only Sunshine. I love you to the Moon and Back. For my Aunt Dottie and my niece Brooke. I love you and miss you both every day and I will see you both again in that sweet by and by. Now let's sit back with a glass of sweet tea and begin, shall we?

Chapter One

I was four years old when I realized I was smart. My mother was always telling everyone how smart I was, but I thought it was just because she liked to be one up on her sister's kids. Her sister, my aunt Joyce, would always say her little Johnny was so bright, and even though he was only two, he already knew his colors, shapes, and several words. I found that hard to believe because all I ever heard him say was "mama" and "I pooped!" Plus he spent an inordinate amount of time with his finger stuck up his nose.

One morning in late August 1961, my mother woke me up and told me to put on my pink pinafore dress and my white sandals and come into the kitchen. I wasn't sure why I was dressing up. I hated wearing dresses. I would much rather wear my Toughskin jeans and a T-shirt. I was particularly fond of my T-shirt that said "Keep on Truckin'," because my daddy drove a big semitruck. When he was home, he would let me talk on his CB radio. My handle was Sunshine, which was also Daddy's nickname for me. I went to the closet and yanked the dress off the hangar. Not only was it a dress, but it was also pink—the horror! I put it on and headed toward the kitchen.

Our housekeeper/cook/nanny/saint, Ernestine, was making biscuits and singing a gospel hymn. Ernestine was my best friend in the whole world, but I knew never to tell mama that. Ernestine had helped raise my mother. My mama's parents were rich, and Ernestine used to work for them. When Mama married my daddy, my grandparents were very upset. Back then, my dad was known as a hell-raiser and liked to drink and chase women. He met my mother at a high school basketball game, and they married three weeks later. When I was born, Ernestine came to live with us to take care of me so Mama could work on getting her figure back and have time for lunches and tennis at the club. My mother's mother was an old-school Southern belle, and she and some other rich women in town had started a "ladies' club" where they could all get together to drink cocktails, lunch, and gossip.

According to my mother my birth was so painful and took so long that she vowed to never have more children. Each time, she told the story my birth took longer and was more painful. If my birth had really taken as long as my mother said, I would have been born potty-trained with a full set of teeth.

Ernestine saw me come into the kitchen and said, "Well, look at this. Where are you going all dolled up?" About that time, my mother breezed into the kitchen. My mother never just walked into a room; she made an entrance.

"Ernestine, coffee and the usual breakfast."

"Yes, ma'am."

Every morning, my mother had a hardboiled egg, a piece of dry toast, and three cups of coffee. When Daddy was gone, she would also have a cigarette after breakfast, but that was a supersecret that I could never tell anyone. I asked her why I had to wear a stupid old dress.

"We are going to the elementary school to enroll you in kindergarten."

"But, Mama, I'm not five, and you have to be five to go to kindergarten." This information had been gleaned from my know-it-all cousin Amanda. She was in the third grade.

"You can start kindergarten when you're four if you know your colors, shapes, and alphabet. You are reading and writing already. I know most of the hillbilly children that go to that school can't do that. You're smart, Christie. Never be ashamed of that. Now go brush your hair and teeth so we can go."

We drove to the school and went into the office. My mother walked up to the counter.

"I would like to speak to Principal Horton, please," my mother said.

The secretary said, "Can I tell him why you would like to meet with him?"

"No."

The secretary blinked her eyes several times very fast.

"Well, can I at least tell him your name?"

My mother let out a big sigh and said, "Betty Lynn Cook."

"Just a moment, please. I will tell him you're here."

The secretary started to type again.

"Were you going to tell him today or do I need to grab a sleeping bag and camp out 'til tomorrow?"

"He's on the phone, Mrs. Cook. I will let him know as soon as he's available."

My mother went and sat down in one of the chairs placed against the wall. I was excited to be starting school. I loved the smell of the school. It smelled like freshly sharpened pencils and old books, two of my favorite smells. I couldn't wait to make friends so I would have someone to play with other than my cousins who my mother said should be riding the short bus. I wasn't sure what that meant, but I knew it had something to do with her thinking they were dumb. My mother had no use for people she felt weren't her intellectual equal.

About that time, the principal walked out of his office, and my mother didn't give the secretary time to announce her; she stood up and went to the principal with her hand out.

"Hello, I'm Betty Lynn Cook. May I speak with you for a moment?"

He shook my mother's hand and asked her to step inside his office.

"C'mon, Christie Ann."

I dutifully walked into the office behind my mother.

"Mrs. Cook, how can I help you?"

"I would like to enroll my daughter in kindergarten."

He looked at me and said, "How old is she?"

"She's four."

"She has to be five to begin kindergarten."

My mother said, "Actually, that's not true. According to the school board, if she knows her colors, numbers, and alphabet, she can start when she is four. She meets the criteria, and she also knows how to read and write."

He looked at me again. "That's wonderful, but we don't feel a four-year-old is emotionally mature enough to be in a classroom."

"I can assure you my daughter is mature enough to hold her own."

He looked at me again. "What's your name, honey?"

My mother looked him in the eye and said, "Don't ever call my daughter honey, sweetie, princess, or any other patronizing name. It's sexist. Her name is Christie."

He swallowed hard and said, "Okay, Christie, I'm going to give you a piece of paper, and I want you to write the alphabet and the numbers one to twenty-five. Can you write your name?"

"Yes, sir. Do you want me to write my whole name or just my first name?"

He blinked fast just like the secretary and told me my first name was fine. I took the piece of paper and did what he asked me to do. I handed the page back to him when I was finished.

"Well, I see you do know your letters and numbers. I'm going to give you a book, and I want you to read the first page. Okay?"

He looked around his office for something to give me to read and couldn't seem to find anything. My mother told him to give me the dictionary and I would read from that. He did the fast eyeblink thing again and handed me the dictionary.

I opened the book to the middle and started reading, "Llama—a South African mammal related to the camel, raised for its soft, fleece wool and used as a beast of burden." I stopped there and looked up. There was the fast blink again.

"Well, it looks like you are a kindergartner, Christie."

I looked at Mama, and she smiled at me. So began my career at Olla Elementary School in Olla, Louisiana. The principal gave my mother a list of supplies I would need and told her to have me at the school at 8:00 a.m. the next morning. I was so excited.

That night, my dad called from the road, and I told him I would be starting kindergarten the next day. He told me to put my mother on the phone. I could only hear her side, but she said, "Nick, she is extremely bright and needs to be in school. She will be fine." Then my mother was silent for a very long time. Then she said, "I made the decision and it's done." She hung up the phone and told me to get ready for bed.

I went into my room and took the clothes out I planned to wear the next day and laid them on the chair in my room. I was going to wear my Levi's and my happy face T-shirt. My mother came in to tell me good night and asked me why the clothes were laid out. I told her because I was wearing them to school the next day. She picked them up, took them to the closet, and hung them back up. She pulled out a navy blue dress with a white collar and laid it on the chair.

"You are wearing this tomorrow."

"Mama, no! I don't want to wear a stinking dress. Everybody will make fun of me."

"Christie Ann, it is not up for discussion. You are not a hillbilly [my mother's word for rednecks and white trash]. I wore dresses to school and so will you. Also, do not share a hairbrush with anyone. I don't want you to catch lice." She kissed me on the forehead and walked out of the room.

I didn't want to wear a dress, but I was still excited about starting school. My mother had been teaching me for the last year, and she became easily frustrated if I didn't quickly grasp the subject. She was also known to use the ruler on the back of my hands if I became tired or whiny. Hopefully, my new teacher wouldn't have a ruler.

The next morning, I was up before Mama. I put the stupid dress on and skipped into the kitchen. Ernestine was mixing up something in a bowl.

"Ernestine, guess what. I'm a kindergartner!"

"I know child. Your Mama told me. I think it's a bad idea, but she don't listen to me. Never has."

"Why is it a bad idea? I think it's a great idea!"

"Ms. Christie, you ain't never had bad luck. All your life, you've been taught you are smarter than all the other kids and you are better than everybody else. People don't like hearing that. I don't know if you're ready for the real world."

I didn't reply because my mother blew through the door into the kitchen.

"Good morning, Ernestine. The usual, please."

I wasn't sure why my mother told Ernestine the same thing every morning. We all knew what she had for breakfast. It never changed. I think she just liked to feel like she was in charge. After breakfasting, my mother took me to school and walked me to my classroom, carrying all my supplies. I had a baby blue book sack on my shoulder full of newly sharpened pencils and notebooks with my name printed inside. I felt like jumping up and down. We walked into my classroom, and all the other kids were sitting in their seats. Everyone turned to look at me. My teacher, Mrs. Nelson, walked over to us.

"You must be Christie. I'm so happy to have you in my class."

My mother handed her the sack of supplies, told me to have a good day, and walked out. All the other kids, including the girls, were dressed in jeans and T-shirts. I was the only one wearing a dress. One of the boys said, "She's a baby! Look at that dress." Everyone laughed. Mrs. Nelson told them to be quiet and walked me to my desk by the window. It was my first day of school.

Chapter Two

I found school to be very boring. My class was learning how words made sentences, and I already knew how to do that. I was always the first one to finish my worksheets. The other kids called me "smarty-pants" and "poop head." All the kids seemed to be fascinated with poop and passing gas. I was taught those were private things and shouldn't be discussed in mixed company. The boys made fart noises with their armpits, which they found hilarious. I had been a kindergartner for three months and still didn't have any friends.

One gray November morning, there was a knock on the classroom door. I looked up and Mr. Horton walked in with a girl who had black curls that looked like they hadn't been brushed in a month of Sundays. She was wearing a T-shirt that was stretched out at the neck and a pair of blue jeans with holes in the knee. She didn't have a coat. Mrs. Nelson introduced her to the class. Her name was Emma Kay Bradford. The teacher told her to take the desk next to mine. Then she told us to take out a blank piece of paper. Emma raised her hand.

"Yes, Emma," Mrs. Nelson said.

"I ain't got no paper."

"I don't have any paper," Mrs. Nelson said.

Emma looked confused. "You don't got no paper either? But you're the teacher."

Mrs. Nelson opened her mouth and then closed it again. "Christie, could you please loan Emma a piece of paper?"

I reached into my notebook and tore out a piece of paper and handed it to her. She mumbled thanks. Mrs. Nelson walked over and handed her a pencil.

"Okay, class, write down as many words as you can think of, and then write the numbers one through twenty-five."

I let out a big sigh. This was so easy. I was on my second page of words when I looked over at Emma's paper. It was blank. She cut her eyes at me and then moved her arm to cover the page so I couldn't see it. I raised my hand.

"Yes, Christie?"

"Emma's page is blank. I don't think she knows how to spell."

Emma looked at me and said under her breath, "When we go out for recess, I'm gonna kick your ass."

"That will be enough!" Mrs. Nelson said. "Emma, we do not use that kind of language in this classroom, and we certainly don't hit each other. Apologize to Christie."

Emma looked down at the floor and said, "Sorry."

The bell rang for lunch, and I started walking toward the cafeteria with everyone else. Someone behind me grabbed my hair and pulled hard. I turned quickly around, but the Robbins twins were the only kids behind me. They were giggling. I started walking faster until I reached the cafeteria where I grabbed a tray and went through the line. We were having fish sticks. I hated fish sticks. I wished I could bring my lunch from home, but Mama said that was common and we certainly had enough money for me to have a balanced meal. I wasn't sure which one of the food groups fish sticks fell into, but they were gross. After I went through the line, I started walking to the back of the cafeteria where I usually sat.

I passed the bad kid's table, and somebody stuck out their foot and tripped me. My tray went flying, and I went to my knees. Everybody started laughing, and I started crying. Then they started chanting. "Crybaby, crybaby." I got to my feet and ran outside. I hated school! I hadn't learned one new thing and hadn't made any friends, and now everyone was laughing at me. I wanted to go home and play Civil War with Ernestine. Mr. McDowell, the hall monitor came outside and asked me what happened. I told him, and he patted me on the back and said that I was having a bad day, but it would pass. The kids would forget about me in a day or two, and everything would be fine. I hoped he was right.

When Mama picked me up from school, she asked me how I skinned my knee. I told her I fell playing. She said we would put some Mercurochrome on it when we got home. I wasn't sure, but I knew not to tell Mama the other kids were picking on me, so I told her about Emma and how we were friends and ate lunch together. That made her happy. I knew enough by the age of four to know that keeping my mother happy was paramount over everything else. I decided to just suck it up and try to get through the rest of the year.

Things did not improve at school. Emma had it out for me, and though she never hit me, she made my life miserable. She called me Goody Two-shoes and told everyone I thought I was better than them. She would follow me into the bathroom, stand outside the door, and call me names like snot licker and booger eater. I never cried again, but I felt so alone. There was no one I could talk to except Ernestine. She told me that the other kids were just jealous and to ignore them. That was easier said than done. School was almost out, and I still hadn't learned anything new except how to cuss. One night at dinner, my parents were arguing, and my dad said, "You win Betty Lynn. You're always right. I don't even know why I try to voice my opinion."

I said, "Yeah, Daddy, you better be good, or she will kick your ass." That got me sent to the bathroom where I had to hold a bar of soap in my mouth for five minutes and then go to bed without dessert.

Sometimes when I was taking my bath, I would say all the bad words out loud where Mama couldn't hear me. Saying those words made me feel older, so I started using them at school. The other kids thought it was funny and would put me up to saying all the cuss words at once—piss, shit, damn, hell. At least they were laughing with me now instead of at me. Emma got bored with teasing me and started picking on another girl in class who had a lisp. I feared Emma, but I was also fascinated by her. She didn't care what other people thought. I longed for that type of freedom.

Finally, school was out, and Mrs. Nelson recommended that I skip a grade and go into second grade at the beginning of the school year. Luckily, Daddy put his foot down and said no. That didn't stop Mama from telling everyone the teacher wanted me to skip a grade.

The summer between kindergarten and first grade, my grandfather was murdered. He was my daddy's daddy. I had only seen him twice. He liked to drink whiskey, and my mother thought he was a bad influence on me, so he didn't come around much. The last time I saw him, he asked me if I had a piggy bank. I ran into the house and grabbed my ceramic piggy bank out of my room. I took it out to the porch and showed it to him. He said, "Well, let's see if we can fill it up a little." He emptied all the change he had in his pockets onto the porch. I looked at him with wide eyes.

"Is that for me?"

"Yes, child. Put it in your bank."

I yelled, "Thank you," hugged his neck, and began to pick up the change and put it in my bank. He chuckled and told me I was a pretty little girl. He told me I looked just like my daddy, but everyone said that. I didn't know why Mama didn't like him. I thought he was great.

I didn't know what the word murder meant, but one night while Mama and Daddy were talking, I heard my daddy say, "He beat him in the head with a hammer. He was so drunk; he couldn't even defend himself." I snuck back into my room and cried into my pillow. When I became an adult, I requested the police report and autopsy report regarding my grandfather. He was at twice the legal limit of intoxication when a man in his rooming house beat him to death with a hammer over a card game. There was also a sheet of information from the army. He served in World War II and stormed the beach at Normandy. He was a hero. I wish I knew what happened between being a hero and becoming an alcoholic who was murdered in his own bed.

Mama wouldn't let me go to the funeral. She thought I was too young, so I stayed home with Ernestine. We were sitting on the front porch swing when I asked her why some people were so mean. She said usually when something bad happens to someone, they become bad to other people. She said people should be careful not to put themselves in a situation where something bad could happen. She said she didn't know why, but some people were just born mean. We sat on the porch swing for a long time, watching the sun go down. It was the first time I knew the world could be a very dangerous place, and there were people who could hurt you for no reason at all.

That was also the summer Jimmy came to visit his grandparents. They lived next door to us. I loved Mr. and Mrs. Snoddy. Thursday was Mrs. Snoddy's baking day, and she would always call me over to try whatever scrumptious dessert she had made. She told me about her grandson, Jimmy, who was my age and lived in Houston, Texas. She said he was smart, and she bet we would get along "like a house afire." That was also the summer my mother signed me up for the Brownies, which were basically baby Girl Scouts. We wore dresses, practiced setting a table and folding napkins, and learned how to manage the help. I hated it and all the girls that were in it. They were all snooty, never got dirty, and wore ribbons in their hair that matched their dresses. Mama set up a few play dates for me and the other girls, but I always ended up hanging out with their brothers, blowing up Barbie dolls with firecrackers and hanging lizards from my ears. At least once a week, my mother would ask Daddy where she went wrong.

Unless you have lived it, you have no idea how hot it is in Louisiana during the summer. It's humid and the air is so heavy; you lose your breath when you walk outside. You immediately start sweating, and once that happens, the mosquitoes attack. They buzz around your ears and dive-bomb your head. There is no bug spray that can kill them. There are also fire ants. They build ant hills in the yard, and if you make the mistake of stepping on their hill, they sting you. If that happens, the bites will turn red and you have to take medicine. I tried not to go outside during the summer, or if I did, I stayed on the porch. I also refused to wear anything except my bathing suit.

I was lying on the porch swing one cloudy afternoon reading a book. I had finished the Laura Ingalls Wilder books, and now I was reading Nancy Drew. I liked the Hardy Boys better, but Mama wouldn't let me read those. She said they were for boys. I saw movement out of the corner of my eye and looked over the top of my book. I saw a skinny boy walking down the gravel road toward our house. He was wearing shorts, a short-sleeved dress shirt tucked into his shorts, black socks, and church shoes.

"Hey! Who are you?" I yelled.

He jumped like he had been shot and screamed.

I had never heard a boy scream before. My boy cousins were mean as snakes and made it their life's work to terrorize me and my girl cousins Susie and Deann. I wasn't accustomed to boys who screamed.

"Are you Christie?"

"Yep. Who are you?"

"My name's Jimmy. I'm the Snoddy's grandson. They said you might want to play with me."

"I guess. You wanna walk down to the creek? We haven't had much rain so it's pretty low, but we can catch crawdads?"

"Okay."

I grabbed my bucket from the back porch and yelled to my mother that I was going to the creek and ran to catch up with Jimmy. We didn't talk as we walked through the woods. We were too busy trying to slap off the mosquitoes.

"Good lord. These mosquitoes are huge. You got any bug spray?" Jimmy said.

"Bug spray doesn't work on these skeeters. They just keep right on biting. The only thing that works is Skin So Soft from Avon, but we're all out and Mama hasn't bought anymore."

We finally made it to the creek, but the water level was so low that you could see the bottom. I walked over and looked; all I could see was mud. I walked down a little farther and saw where some water had pooled between two fallen trees. I grabbed a stick and started poking at the logs.

"What are you doing?"

"Making sure there aren't any snakes."

"There are snakes out here?" Jimmy's voice was very high.

"Uh, yeah. They like to hide under trees in the water."

About that time, a water moccasin slithered out from under the tree I was hitting. I was wearing my rubber boots, so I just walked backward very slowly. The snake went into the grass and on his way, looking for another dark, wet place to hide.

"Yeah, I don't think this is a good idea. I don't want to get snake bit" Jimmy said.

"Do you want to play Civil War?" I asked.

"How do you play that?"

"Well, I'm always Robert E. Lee. You can be Stonewall Jackson. We shoot Yankees and let the slaves go."

"I don't think that's what happened."

"Yes, it is. I play it all the time."

"I don't want to play that. It sounds boring. What else is there to do? Is there a movie theater around here?"

"Not unless we go to Alec and that's an hour away. We can shoot cans with my BB gun."

"Okay."

"Have you ever shot a gun?"

"No," Jimmy said.

I took a deep breath. I was going to have to turn Jimmy into a boy or it would be a long summer.

Chapter Three

The summer rolled along. We had a week of rain, and the creek filled up. Jimmy and I spent a lot of time down there fishing and swimming. I had to teach him how to put the worm on the hook. When he saw the guts, he started gagging. I taught him how to shoot a BB gun. He wasn't very good, but he hit a can every now and then. We talked about his dad quite a bit. Jimmy's daddy was a businessman who lived in California. Jimmy only saw him once a year at Christmas. His daddy was remarried, so Jimmy had a stepmother. He hated her. He also had a half brother that was two years old. Jimmy said all he did was sleep, poop, and annoy him. I think deep down he really liked him because he talked about him a lot. He said the good thing about having divorced parents was you get two of everything—two birthdays, two Christmases—and if he asked his mom for something and she said no, he would just call his dad and his dad would send him whatever he wanted. I decided I was going to try to make Mama and Daddy get a divorce.

Over the summer, Daddy got a new job, working at a pipe terminal where he was the boss. I was excited because that meant he would be home at night. He had a secretary named Sue. She was pretty and would always give me gum when I would go visit Daddy. I'm not sure what happened to her, but one day when I went into his office, she was gone and an old woman smoking a cigarette was at her desk. Her name was Marjorie, but my dad called her Sue. He said he didn't have time to learn a new name. Marjorie was the first of a long line of Sue's. Finding someone my mother approved of who could type was difficult. Finally, my mother decided that she would just do the job herself. That worked about as well as putting two cats in a feed sack.

My mother volunteered at the church twice a week, so on those days, I rode the bus to my dad's office. I loved his office. He would let me sit in his chair and play with the typewriter. My mother would usually arrive around 4:00 p.m. As soon as she walked in, she would start griping at my dad about something. I knew my dad wanted her to stop working for him, but he wasn't sure how to fire her. Luckily, he didn't have to. One day, my dad's boss stopped by the office and made the mistake of calling my mother honey and telling her to make him a cup of coffee. I wasn't sure what she said to him, but my dad received a phone call the next day, telling him either my mother had to go or he did. My mother never got over the fact my dad fired her. She would often bring it up when they were arguing.

Before I knew it, summer ended, and it was time to go back to school. Jimmy went back to Houston, promising to write letters. The first day back at school, I noticed a girl that I had never seen before. She was tiny. Her clothes were out-of-date and faded. Her hair hung in her face. It was tangled and looked greasy. I decided at that moment, she was going to be my pet project. Her name was Laura.

I liked first grade much better than kindergarten. My teacher gave me different worksheets than the other kids. I was learning multiplication tables and how to write stories while the other kids worked on simple math and how to develop a sentence. My teacher said my stories were entertaining and I might grow up to be another Harper Lee. I loved Harper Lee. She was my favorite author. My cousin Rebecca who was fourteen had to read *To Kill a Mockingbird* for school. I asked her what it was about, and she told me I wasn't old enough to read it. The next day, I walked to the local library after school and checked out a copy. I told the librarian it was for my mother. When I got home, I told my mother I was going to play in my room. I dug out one of my Dr. Seuss books and put *To Kill a Mockingbird* inside. That way, if Mama came in, she wouldn't be able to see what I was really reading. I opened the book and began to read.

There were some parts I didn't understand, like the word rape. I had no idea what it meant, but I knew it was bad. I also realized that being a black person in the South was no picnic. The book also used the *n* word a lot. My mother told me not to ever use that word. She said it was common. My uncle Joe was at our house one day, and he said the *n* word. My mother told him that every time he said that word, his IQ dropped ten points. He left soon after.

After reading the book, I knew what I wanted to be when I grew up. I wanted to be a writer like Harper Lee.

First grade was also the year that "the flip-flop incident" occurred. On the weekends, Daddy liked to work on the car and drink a few beers. I would always follow him around and hand him the tools he needed. One Saturday, I was sitting on the grass by the driveway reading *Where the Red Fern Grows* while Daddy changed the oil in mama's car. Daddy's voice came out from under the car and said, "Did you know I invented flip-flops?" I looked over, and all I could see were his legs stretched out in front of the car.

"Really?" I said.

"Yep. When I was about your age, we were so poor. I didn't have any shoes. We had some old tires behind the house, so I cut one up and grabbed some rope, tied it to the tire rubber, and used it for shoes. Flip-flops were born."

I thought about it for a minute. "Daddy, if you invented flip-flops, why aren't we rich?" He said something about not getting a patent and some "sum-bitch" beating him to the punch. The next day, I went to school and repeated the story verbatim at lunch. One of the playground monitors overheard the story including the "sum-bitch" part and sent me to the office. They called my mother.

I was sitting in the office when my mother blew in and grabbed me by my upper arm. She told the secretary she was taking me home to "have a talk with me." When we got in the car, she said, "Why on earth would you tell everybody your daddy invented flip-flops?" I told her what daddy had told me, but this time, I left the cuss word out. She took me straight to daddy's office where she went in, slammed his door, and started yelling. My mother was embarrassed, but my daddy thought it was hilarious. After Mama stopped yelling,

Daddy told me to come in his office. He told me he had been teasing me and that he really didn't invent flip-flops. That was my first lesson in the difference between the truth and a lie.

My mother decided I was too much of a tomboy, and she set out to change me. She was determined I was going to be a girl if it killed us both. She had an uphill battle. My father had always wanted a boy, and my mother said she was never having any more children because of all the pain she went through giving birth to me. It was my father's mission in life to make me the biggest tomboy in LaSalle Parish. For my fifth birthday, he bought me a BB gun; and on the weekends, we would go out in the woods and shoot cans. He taught me how to play poker and pool and to stand up for myself. I wore Levi's and denim shirts and cowboy boots. My mother tried everything she could think of to turn me into a lady.

Mama woke up one morning and decided she was going to redecorate my room. She made me sleep on the couch for a month because she didn't want me to see it until she was finished. The big day finally arrived, and my mother told me and my dad to come down the hall. She was standing in front of my bedroom door. She opened the door and shouted, "Ta-da!" I walked into the room and felt my stomach drop. The room was painted a very light pink, and there was a canopy bed whose cover matched the curtains and the bedspread. There were white rugs on the floor, and she had dug out my dolls of every nation and placed them on a shelf above the bed.

"Wow, this is really something," my dad said.

"Well, what do you think? I saw it in a magazine," my mom asked.

I looked at Daddy, and he subtly shook his head.

"I love it," I said.

My mother grabbed me by my arm and pulled me into the room excitedly talking, telling me how she went to the fabric store and picked out the pattern and that she and Ernestine sewed everything themselves. I asked my parents if I could have some time to myself to enjoy all the changes. They went out and quietly shut the door. I could still hear my mother talking excitedly as they walked down the hall. My heart dropped when I heard her say, "The next thing to go will be those cowboy boots."

I sat down on the edge of the bed and looked around. I hated it. The room went against everything I stood for. She had taken my stuffed deer head my grandfather had given me that used to hang over my bed. She took my John Deere tractor sign. My BB gun was in the back of my closet, and all my blue jeans were pushed to the side. I could see new dresses hanging. I felt sick. This was my worst nightmare come true.

There was a soft knock on my door.

"Yeah?"

"Hon, can I come in?" It was Ernestine.

"Yes."

She walked in and sat down beside me on the bed.

"Ernestine, it's horrible. I hate it!"

"I know, honey. The whole time we were sewing, I knew you would hate it."

"Then why didn't you tell her?" I cried.

"Child, you know you can't tell your mama nothing."

"What am I going to do? She's threatening to take away my cowboy boots, and she replaced all my blue jeans with dresses. I hate dresses!"

"Well, there are ways to get around things," Ernestine said.

"What do you mean?"

"Sometimes to get along, we need to make people believe we like something they gave us, or we can have a secret we keep to ourselves like hiding our blue jeans in our book bag and changing when we get to school."

I looked at Ernestine and said, "Wouldn't that be a lie?"

"Well, there are big lies, and then there are little white lies."

Ernestine explained the difference between the two. I started to feel better. I would make Mama think I was becoming a lady, but I would still be Daddy's son.

I hugged Ernestine and walked down the hall into the living room. My parents were listening to the LSU/Auburn game on the radio. They both looked up when I walked into the room.

"Okay, I will sleep in the room, and I will wear dresses sometimes, but you aren't taking away my cowboy boots."

Chapter Four

I was in the first grade when my mother signed me up for etiquette lessons. I was five years old. My teacher was Ms. Parker. She was about eighty years old and smoked like a chimney. She coughed constantly, and when the coughing got the best of her, she would take a shot of whiskey she kept in a small glass on the side table. She had never married. Her claim to fame was that her grandfather, John Milliken Parker, was a former governor of Louisiana, and rumor had it that she had been Huey P. Long's mistress until he was murdered by that Jewish doctor. I was terrified of her.

The first three sessions were spent on curtsying. No one I knew curtsied anymore, but she made me practice over and over until I had perfected each step. Lower your head. Bend your head forward slightly, as if giving a respectful nod. Hold your skirt. Extend your right foot behind the left. Bend your knees. Gracefully bring yourself back to your original position. I had the most trouble with the last step. I did not do anything gracefully. My mother said I had a "heavy walk," and she always knew when I was awake just by listening to my walk. Ms. Parker would yell at me, cough, take a slug of whiskey, light another cigarette, and then tell me to do it again. Finally, after three weeks, she was satisfied.

Mother picked me up after the third week, and when I got in the car, she said, "Well, what did you learn today?" I told her I practiced curtsying. She didn't say anything else until we were home.

"Christie Ann, why are you having such a hard time learning to curtsy?"

"I don't know mother. She just doesn't like me. She says I'm uncoordinated."

My mother began to yell, and I decided I was done. I wasn't going to sleep in that room with the pink walls, I wasn't going to wear dresses, and I wasn't going back to see Ms. Parker anymore, ever. I yelled all of this to my mother and ran into my room slamming the door. I pulled out my camouflage duffel bag Daddy had given me and threw in a pair of underwear and my lucky rabbit's foot my grandfather had given me. I zipped the bag and walked down the hall and out the front door, slamming it behind me. I stood on the porch for a couple of minutes to see if Mama would come after me, but the door remained closed. We lived down a long, gravel road that led to the highway into town. I started walking. My grandma lived downtown, and I thought I remembered how to get to her house. About that time, I saw Daddy's old red Chevrolet truck rolling toward me. When he was even with me, he rolled down his window.

"Where you headed, Sunshine?"

"Mamaw's."

"Uh-huh. What's in the bag?"

"My unmentionables."

That's what my mother always said if Daddy needed to find something in her purse and she didn't want him to. She was afraid he would see her cigarettes.

"I see. Is there a particular reason you're running away?"

"Yeah. Mama's trying to turn me into a girl!"

I saw him start to smile, and then he caught himself.

"Well, why don't you climb in here with me, and we will go to the Burger Barn for a hot fudge sundae?"

I thought about it for a minute. I really wanted a hot fudge sundae, but I also wanted to make my point.

"C'mon. I'll talk to your mama."

I was glad Daddy found me before I walked any further. It was November and cold, and I had forgotten my coat. When we got to the Burger Barn, purchased our sundaes, and sat down in one of the red plastic booths, Daddy went to call Mama to let her know I was safe. When he came back and sat down, I asked him why Mama got mad at me when I did boy things.

He took a deep breath and told me how Mama had never had anything bad happen to her. Her parents kept her sheltered and wouldn't even let her read the newspaper or watch the news because she might read or hear something that would upset her. He said when Mama married him, my grandparents were really upset and tried to talk Mama out of it. Mama had been dating a local boy who was in medical school at LSU. My grandparents wanted Mama to marry him. Daddy said Mama's parents loosened up a little when I was born. He said Mama wanted me to be a "Southern belle," like her mama. He said she felt like she had to prove marrying my dad wasn't a mistake and by turning me into the perfect little girl, she would win. He said she always had to win. I continued eating my sundae and thought about what Daddy said.

"I guess I could act like a girl sometimes," I said.

He smiled. "That would make your mother happy."

As we were leaving, Daddy told me not to ever run away again because "some sick sum-bitch" could have picked me up instead. I promised I wouldn't.

When we got home, Mama was sitting on the front porch swing, knitting with an old quilt wrapped around her. She didn't lift her head to look at me when I walked up the stairs to the front porch. My dad said hello and gave her a kiss. I stood in front of her. I told her I was sorry. Daddy made me do that. My mother looked up, and I could see she had been crying. I wasn't immediately concerned because my mother could cry at the drop of a hat, usually to get her way about something.

"How could my daughter, who I put all my energy and attention into, yell at me and then run away and worry me sick? How can my daughter, who I gave up my career for, completely and totally disrespect me? How? I ask you."

I wasn't sure what career she was talking about. When my mother got pregnant with me she was working as a clerk at Don's Hardware Store. She quit as soon as she started showing. One time, I heard her tell my aunt Dottie that she was being considered for an office manager position when she left, but she gave it all up so she could stay home and raise me.

I always thought that was interesting because Mama spent very little time with me. If I was hurt or scared and Daddy wasn't home, I went to Ernestine. The only attention I received from Mama was on Sundays. We went to church with her parents, my grandparents, and then back to their house for lunch. Mama took extra care with my appearance on those Sundays. She curled my hair and put me in a dress that I wore with white knee socks and my black patent leather shoes.

While we were eating lunch, she would focus on me. She bragged that I was on the A honor roll and was the teacher's little helper. I'm not sure where she got that information. I had a B in math, and I helped the teacher dust erasers once. The chalk dust went into my throat and up my nose. I started gagging and told the teacher I felt faint. (That was another one of Mama's tactics that she used when she didn't want to deal with something; she fake fainted.) My teacher told me to get a drink from the water fountain and then go back to class. Mama also liked to bring up the fact that I went to kindergarten when I was four. She always figured out a way to include it in the conversation.

Daddy didn't attend church or the Sunday lunches. My grandmother would tersely ask me how my father was doing. I would tell her fine, and then we went about our business. I loved my grandparents. They gave nice presents on my birthday, but going to their house was so boring. After everyone had lunch and the women cleaned up, we all retired to the living room to read or nap. Mama always brought me baby books that I had read a hundred times. The adults had coffee, and I was allowed a glass of milk and a slice of one of grandma's pies or cakes. My grandmother made the best pies and cakes in LaSalle Parish. She had won ribbons at the fair for her rhubarb pie.

My grandparents owned a farm, and my grandfather planted cotton. My grandfather was also a forklift operator at the local paper plant. My grandmother said he was a "gentleman farmer," which meant laborers did all the work and he cashed the checks—at least that's what Daddy said. My grandfather had 2,500 acres, and when the crop was ready, I helped the workers pick the cotton. I had to wear gloves because the cotton is inside a little pocket that has stickers on the outside. If you weren't careful, those little stickers would open your finger, and it really, really hurt. My grandparents hired black people to help pick the cotton. I loved to be in the field when the helpers were there. They always sang songs while they were working, mostly church hymns.

I went to church with Ernestine several times, and her church was so much fun. People clapped, put their hands in the air, and praised the Lord. I loved it. Our church was boring. We were Southern Baptist, and we weren't allowed to do anything. You couldn't drink or smoke or dance or anything else fun. My grandmother had a drink once a year at Christmas. She made homemade eggnog with whiskey in it, and she would have a glass before dinner. She was so worried about the neighbors finding out; she would wrap the whiskey bottle in a brown paper bag and then put it at the bottom of a garbage bag before she threw it out. Daddy said he didn't go to church because everyone there was a hypocrite. My dad wanted to be Catholic. He said you could do anything you wanted as long as you went to Mass and confessed. He said they even drank wine during the service. He said it sounded like his kind of place. My mother said Catholicism was a cult.

Every summer, I went to my grandparents for three weeks. My grandmother said it was to give Mama a break to "settle her nerves." My grandparents were big on manners. When I was around them, I had to say yes ma'am and no ma'am and please and thank-you. My grandmother was also a strict disciplinarian. If you did something she thought was rude or common, she would make you go out to the little tree in the front yard and choose a switch. If the switch was flimsy, she made you go out and get another one, and she added a lick to your punishment. I had never had to get my own switch.

My grandmother had the rule book in her head, and I was not a party to that information, so I just minded my manners and tried to stay out of her way. One time, she told me to go to the chicken yard and gather the eggs. I was reading, so I told her I would in a minute.

Before I knew what was happening, she had me over her knee and was hitting my behind with her hand. With each lick, she would tell me that I better not ever tell her to wait a minute. She gave me three licks and sent me to the spare bedroom until I was ready to apologize. I didn't cry. I was in shock. I knew she spanked my cousins—a lot—but she had never laid a hand on me. I didn't come out until it was suppertime. When we were all seated at the table, I said, "Grandma, I'm sorry I sassed you today."

She said, "Apology accepted," and that was it. She never hit me again.

Chapter Five

Laura and I started sitting together at lunch and playing together at recess. Finally, in February, I convinced Mama to let me have Laura over to spend the night. I was so excited. Ernestine made her special Italian wedding cookies and homemade lemonade. Laura wasn't a girly girl either. I had our whole day planned out. Daddy was going to take us fishing at the creek. Then we were going to the A&W to get ice-cream floats; then Daddy was taking us to the Strand in Alexandria to see Bambi.

On the day of Laura's visit, I couldn't sit still. Mama finally told me to go wait on the front porch. I was sitting on the swing when Laura's dad's truck pulled up in front of our house. It sounded like the muffler had fallen off, and there was Bondo on the front and back side panels. Laura got out of the truck, carrying a plastic grocery bag with her things in it. Mama was standing at the screen door, and I heard her say, "Dear Lord." I ran down the steps to meet Laura. We hugged and then laughed. I grabbed her hand and pulled her into the house to meet Mama and Daddy. My mother greeted her in her company voice.

"Well, hello, Laura! We are so happy to have you. Can I take your bag?"

Laura looked at the floor and shook her head no. Mother looked at me, and her lips were in a line. She said, "Well, I will leave you girls to it," and walked into the sitting room.

Daddy walked over and stuck out his hand. "Hi, Laura, how are you?" Laura didn't shake Daddy's hand. She mumbled fine and continued to look at the floor.

"Well," Daddy said, "who's ready to go fishing?"

I started jumping up and down. "Me, me!" I yelled. We walked around the house to the shed and took out fishing rods and the tackle box. Daddy had stopped by the gas station that morning and bought worms. I looked in the container and saw them squirming around. I didn't like sticking the hooks in the worms because I believed that every living thing felt pain, but I understood the worms had to be sacrificed to catch fish. We started walking toward the creek, and Laura pulled my arm. I stopped and leaned in to hear her. "I don't have any more shoes. I can't get these wet." I didn't know what to say. Mama bought me a new pair of shoes every time she went to town. Some of them I had never worn. I told Laura it was fine. She could borrow a pair of mine. She smiled, and we kept walking.

"So, Laura, what does your dad do?" Daddy asked.

Laura looked confused for a minute and then said, "Mostly, he just sits on the sofa drinking beer."

Daddy coughed and then said, "I mean what does he do for a job?"

"He doesn't have a job. He hurt his back working in the warehouse at Woolworths. Now he gets disability. My mom is a housekeeper at the Doe Inn out on the highway. She works at night and sleeps all day."

"Do you have brothers or sisters?" Daddy asked.

"I have one brother, but he's in juvenile detention in Grayson. He stole money from the Five and Dime Store."

Daddy coughed again and said, "Well, let's catch some fish."

We had a great time, and Laura caught four fish. She asked Daddy if she could take them home with her the next day. She wanted to cook them for supper. I couldn't believe she was only six and could cook. I could barely pour my own milk. Ernestine did all the cooking at our house.

After we finished fishing, we loaded up in Daddy's truck and went to the A&W for root beer floats. Laura had never had one before. Several times, I caught Daddy looking at Laura in a sad way. When she went to the bathroom, I asked him why he kept staring at her.

"That child doesn't have a chance in hell."

I wanted to ask him what he meant, but Laura came back to the truck, and it was time to go to the movie. Laura had never been to a movie either, and Daddy let us get popcorn and candy. I had seen the movie before, and I knew what happened to Bambi's mother, but it still made me sad. Laura cried at the part when Bambi's mother got shot. She was still crying when we left the theater, and she cried all the way home. Daddy and I kept looking at each other and raising our eyebrows. When we got home, Laura and I went into my room to play a game. We chose Operation and sat down on the floor. Laura looked around and said, "You are so lucky."

I had never really thought about it, but she was right. I had never been poor or hungry. My Mama was a pain in the butt, but she loved me. I had Daddy and Ernestine and all my cousins, grandparents, and aunts and uncles who loved me. If I wanted something, Daddy would buy it for me. Now that I thought about it, I was lucky. I didn't know what to say to Laura, so I told her she could go first. We played games until it was time for supper; then we caught fireflies in a jar, took our baths, and went to bed.

Laura's daddy picked her up the next morning. I knew when she left that something between us had changed. I didn't think we would be sitting together at lunch anymore. Our lives were just too different. Laura had been my first real friend, and when I was older, I would think of her often and wonder what her life had become. I thought the odds of her life, changing for the better, were probably slim, but I still hoped.

Soon after, I became friends with Cherie Brewer. Her dad owned the hardware store where my mother had her "career." I thought she was too girly at first, but once I got to know her, I found out she liked to get dirty and do "boy things" too. We stayed friends until she died of breast cancer at the age of forty-two. I was beside her bed with her family, and I watched as her husband held her hand while the light in her eyes slowly went out.

Chapter Six

Time continued in that slow deliberate way it does when you're a child. It was rare for the temperature to drop below sixty-five degrees in the winter in the South. I remember the weather of my childhood to be hot and sticky or cold and damp. I was six and in the second grade, and John F. Kennedy had been president for almost three years. I liked to listen to him talk. I thought his accent was funny. My parents were dyed-in-the-wool Republicans, but they had both voted for President Kennedy. It was another secret in our family, kind of like mama's smoking. I think my mother voted for Kennedy because he was young and handsome, and she revered his wife. She would always say, "He's Catholic, but I won't hold that against him."

After the election was over, my class spent a month learning about the president, which was unheard of because when you grow up in the South, you don't learn about American History or European History; you learn about one thing and one thing only, the civil war, or as my family calls it, the War of Northern Aggression. I remember my grandfather talking to one of his friends telling him he was twenty-one years old before he knew damn, and Yankee were two separate words. I don't know if I remembered it because I had never heard my grandfather cuss before or because I felt it was something important I should know.

We had to make a diorama about President Kennedy, and my mother wanted to help me. It was the only class project I ever remembered her helping with. She cut pictures out of magazines, which consisted mostly of Jackie Kennedy, and helped me paste them into the shoebox. She found a picture of the White House, cut it out, and put cardboard behind it so it would stand up. It looked nice. I got an A on the project, but my teacher asked if anyone had helped me. I told her no, that I just wanted to do my civic duty as an American citizen. She looked at me for a long moment and then turned back toward the blackboard to begin class for the day.

My birthday was in late November. (The year I was born fell on Thanksgiving. My aunt Elaine always said, "There was no turkey that year.") My cousin Deann had a dollhouse, and when we would go to her house, we would always play with it. I was fascinated by the little family who lived in the house and all the tiny furniture. I decided I had to have one of my own.

I started dropping hints to Mama and Daddy. Mama was thrilled because a dollhouse was something girls played with. I told her that I didn't want a mama or a daddy doll. I wanted two daddies. She and Daddy looked at each other across the table. My daddy said, "Um, men don't live together." I told him that Uncle Harold and Uncle Wyatt lived together. My mother told me that was different and not to call that man Uncle Wyatt. Then they both started talking about something else at the same time trying to change the subject.

My mother said she and Daddy would see about the dollhouse, but it was a very expensive gift. She always said that, and then she bought me what I wanted. I told her I also wanted a fire truck with a real siren and a Swiss Army knife; she sighed deeply and went into the kitchen.

A few weeks later, I was sitting in class working on my multiplication tables while the other kids learned how to add more than two numbers at a time when the principal came on the intercom and ordered the staff to the auditorium. Mrs. Jefferson told me to come sit at her desk and write down the names of anyone who misbehaved; then she hurried out of the classroom.

I sat at Mrs. Jefferson's desk but soon became bored. I was going through her desk drawers when she rushed back in. She was crying and told us to put our coats on and to either catch our regular bus home or wait for our parents to come pick us up. I gathered my coat and went out front to wait for Mama. When I walked out the front door, she was already there. I climbed into the front seat of our station wagon and asked her what was going on. She was sobbing and told me someone had shot the president. I said, "Is he okay?"

She cried harder and said, "No, honey. He's dead."

I was in shock. How could the handsome man with the funny accent be dead? What was going to happen to his little girl and his little boy, John-John, who liked to hide under his daddy's big desk in the round office?

Mama and I walked into the house, and Daddy and Ernestine were listening to the radio. Ernestine was crying, and Daddy looked shocked and pale. He grabbed me and hugged me for a long time. We listened to the radio, but they just kept saying the same things over and over. The president had been riding in a convertible car with the First Lady sitting next to him. She was wearing a pink suit. They were in Dallas, Texas. They think the person who killed the president shot him from a window in the book depository. I didn't know what a book depository was until Daddy explained it to me.

Later, the radio announcer said a man named Lee Harvey Oswald had been arrested for killing a policeman, and then they found out he had killed the president too. Oswald was an ex-marine, which made Daddy mad because he was a marine too. Mama and Ernestine sat on the couch, holding hands and crying. Finally, as it began to get dark, Daddy said, "C'mon, Ernestine. I'll take you home."

After they left, Mama told me to go get ready for bed. Ernestine had forgotten to give me dinner, but I didn't say anything. I wasn't hungry anyway. I didn't even brush my teeth; I just put my nightgown on and climbed into bed. I thought about that little boy and girl running to meet their dad when his presidential helicopter landed on the lawn at the White House, and I cried myself to sleep.

The next morning, Mama told me to eat a bowl of cereal, and then she wanted to go to the church to pray for the president and his family. I ate my cereal quietly. Mama sat at the table and stared out the window. School was closed for the day. Daddy went to work. He said he needed to keep his mind busy even if he didn't accomplish anything. Ernestine didn't come either. Mama said she needed to be with her family. I knew Ernestine really liked the president because he was trying to give black people more rights. One day when I came home from school, she was really excited because the president had made a speech about how everyone should have the same rights. I didn't understand why some people got so mad about black kids going to school with white kids or black people eating at the same restaurants we went to. My daddy raised me to judge a person by the way they behaved and how they treated other people, not because of the color of their skin.

Mama and I went to church after breakfast, and everyone was there—my grandparents, cousins, aunts, and uncles. All the women were crying, and the men stood in groups talking quietly. Many of the ladies had brought food, but no one was hungry. Daddy showed up about two thirty, and told Mama he was taking me home. We were almost home when I asked Daddy why someone would kill President Kennedy. He didn't say anything for a long time. He finally looked at me and said, "Fear. There is a certain group of people, especially here in the South, who think we should still live on plantations and keep slaves. They are afraid of losing their way of life. Change terrifies them, especially if that changes mean black people will have a voice. They can't seem to get over the fact that we lost the civil war. I think some of them don't realize it's over, and they are just waiting on supplies."

We pulled up in front of our house. Daddy turned off the truck and just sat there looking out the front window. "Christie, a lot of people are cruel and mean. They have black hearts. I've never understood that kind of hate, and I probably never will. It's so much easier to just be kind. Let's go in. What do you want for dinner?"

"Grilled hamburgers," I said.

"You got it."

I went to bed early. Daddy wouldn't let me listen to the radio when we finished dinner. We read *Charlotte's Web* instead even though we had read it together hundreds of times. Daddy always choked up when Charlotte died. I did too. It just seemed like the kind of book we should read that night. Daddy tucked me in and told me how proud he was of me and the young woman I was growing up to be.

He turned out the light and stood at my door for a long time until I finally fell asleep.

The next morning, I went back to school. Right before lunch, the principal came on the intercom and told all the staff to report to the auditorium. Mrs. Jefferson ran out of the room without putting anyone in charge of the class. It didn't matter because we were all too scared to do anything. A little while later, Mrs. Nelson came back and told us school was dismissed for the day. When I walked out front, Daddy was there. When I saw him, I started crying. I ran to him, and he caught me and hugged me. I asked him what had happened. He said a man named Jack Ruby had shot Lee Harvey Oswald. I just looked at him. I knew I shouldn't be happy, but I was. The bad man couldn't hurt anyone else. He was dead. I got in Daddy's truck, and we were both quiet all the way home. Neither of us knew what to say. Mama was resting, so Daddy made me a grilled cheese sandwich and told me to read quietly. I was only six years old, but I knew the world had just changed in a very profound way.

I returned to school the next day, and everyone was subdued. Mrs. Jefferson just handed out worksheets and didn't play any of the math or language arts games we usually played. She forgot to let us out for morning recess until one of the Robbins twins reminded her. By then, recess was almost over. No one felt like playing anyway.

During the afternoon, the school counselor, Ms. Walters, came in and asked us if we had any questions or anything we wanted to talk about. Everyone talked about being scared something might happen to us. What if someone came to the school and shot us. She told us that school was one of the safest places we could be, and no one would ever come into a school and start shooting students. She gave us her word. I asked her what was going to happen to John-John and Caroline. Her eyes welled up with tears and she said, "It will be hard, but they have a great mom and a big family who loves them. They also have the legacy of their father to uphold." I didn't know what the word legacy meant, but it sounded important. She told us we could write Mrs. Kennedy and the children letters, and she would put them all in an envelope and mail them to the White House. Mrs. Jefferson gave us the rest of the afternoon to work on our letters.

I wrote Mrs. Kennedy and told her how pretty I thought she was and how much my mom liked her. I wrote to the children and told them how sorry I was that their daddy was killed by a bad man. I told them that my mama and daddy had voted for their daddy, and we all thought he was a good president. I told them it may not seem like it now, but there was a lot of good in the world; and in the end, it would outshine the bad. I drew a picture of the state of Louisiana with a heart in the middle, signed my name, and put the letter in the envelope Ms. Walters had given us. For the rest of the time before the bell rang, I laid on my desk with my head on top of my arms staring out the window.

My birthday was only four days away, but I just couldn't get excited about it. Things just felt wrong, and I didn't think I should be happy and have a birthday party when Caroline and John-John wouldn't have their daddy anymore. I didn't say anything to Mama and Daddy, but it didn't matter because they forgot my birthday that year. The first week of December, Mama was sitting on the couch when she sat up straight and said, "Oh my god. We forgot Christie Ann's birthday!" Daddy grabbed me, hugged me, and started apologizing. They told me I could have anything I wanted for Christmas, so I told them I wanted a dollhouse and a puppy. I knew I wouldn't get a puppy because Mama was allergic, but I thought this was probably the best time to ask. They both promised me I would have an amazing Christmas.

A few days later after school, I walked outside to catch the bus. Mama was waiting for me on the sidewalk in front of the school. She had been extremely nice to me since she realized she had forgotten my birthday. I was milking it for all it was worth.

"Mama, what are you doing here?"

"Can't a mother pick her child up from school without getting the third degree? I was at the club playing Bridge with the girls when Dottie started cheating. I usually let it slide, but this time, I called her out on it. She got mad and accused me of cheating, so I gathered up my things and left. I thought I would pick you up on the way home."

Everyone who had ever played any type of game with my mother knew she was a big cheat. When I was little and we would play Candy Land, she would always move her piece extra spaces so she could win. My dad and I knew what a sore loser she was, so we just ignored it when she took extra money when she passed go in Monopoly. The alternative to letting her win was so much worse. She would stomp out of the room and sulk for hours. It was easier to just let it go. My grandfather told me once that my mother had to be the prettiest, smartest person in the room, and she always had to win. He told me my life would go a lot smoother if I kept that in mind. He also told me Daddy should be canonized as a saint for living with my mother without strangling her. That was the only nice thing I ever remembered my grandfather said about my father.

"Do you want to go to the Burger Barn for a hot fudge sundae?" Mama chirped.

"Okay, who are you and where is my mother?" I asked.

"Christie Ann, you act like I never do anything nice for you."

My mother did nice things for me, but usually, they were things that she could brag about or show off, like dressing me up for church and the holidays or making me recite the fifty states and their capitals when company came over. I don't think there was a person in LaSalle Parish who hadn't heard about me starting school at the age of four. She wasn't a hot fudge sundae kind of Mom. Besides, hot fudge sundaes were mine and Daddy's thing. We went to the Burger Barn almost every Saturday afternoon. The owner, Mr. Poole, always gave me extra whip cream. However, I wasn't going to turn down ice cream.

"I would love to go have a hot fudge sundae."

"No, you've ruined it now. I'll take you home," Mama said.

I heaved a big sigh and climbed in the car. Trying to navigate my mother's moods was like trying to sidestep cow patties at a cattle auction. Daddy was always telling her she was crazy. She said poor people were crazy. She was eccentric. She was always trying new things and would change her mind at a moment's notice.

One day, she was going to take art classes, then she decided to be a poet, but she couldn't think of enough words that rhymed so she stopped. She decided she was going to have a garden and "put up" all the vegetables to use in soups and stews during the winter.

When she realized she would have to get down on her knees and put her hands in the dirt, she nixed that. She was currently trying to sale Tupperware to all the women at the club. She held parties, but I believe the main reason the women came was because Mama served fondue and Singapore slings. I remember coming home several afternoons to a houseful of drunk women telling me how cute I was and how much I looked like my daddy. I don't remember people buying much Tupperware, but they sure did enjoy the parties.

Chapter Seven

Before I knew it, school was out for the Christmas holidays. My mother loved Christmas and would decorate every room in the house, including the bathrooms. Daddy said it was hard to do his business with Rudolph, "the Red-Nosed Reindeer," staring at him. We lived in an antebellum home that had been built in 1873. There were always carpenters and painters in our house. Our house was on the tour of homes that the Garden Club held for the holidays each year. In the weeks leading up to the event, Mama would work me and Daddy almost to death. She wanted to make sure everything was perfect. It was exhausting. Finally, the day would come, and mother would wear her Scarlett O'Hara dress and stand in the foyer welcoming everyone. Of course, they all complimented her on how beautifully the house was decorated and how lovely she looked, just like a real Southern belle. Mama ate it up.

I hated the home tour because I had to wear a fancy dress and walk around, offering people cookies. Carrying a silver tray full of cookies around for hours was tiresome and boring. People kept telling me how pretty I was and what a good girl I was to help my mother. I gave them my fake smile and kept moving.

Finally, it was over, and we could enjoy Christmas as a family. We always spent Christmas Eve with Daddy's mama, and that to me was the most fun part of Christmas. I played outside with my cousins. Winter in Louisiana is notoriously mild, and each year, my grandmother would cook turkey and dressing, fresh vegetables from her garden, mashed potatoes and gravy, and, for dessert, Heavenly Hash cake. The cake was my favorite thing about going to her house.

The men would sneak out behind grandma's shed and take big sips of whiskey. The women drank fuzzy navels and vodka tonics.

It was great because the adults got tipsy and let us kids do whatever we wanted. My grandmother didn't have much money, so the family drew names, and there was a five-dollar limit on gifts. I would always pray one of my cousins would draw my name so I would get something really cool like a whoopee cushion or a spider encased in plastic. For the last three years, my aunt Jeanette had pulled my name, and she always gave me socks. Hopefully, this year would be different.

We had a great time at my grandma's, and before I knew it, Daddy was packing everything up to leave. My eyes were heavy, and I was ready for my bed. My aunt Bobby had drawn my name, and she gave me a cap gun. I was thrilled, but Mama grabbed it and told me she would hold it for me until I was a little older. I knew I would never see it again. I didn't remember Daddy carrying me to the truck or into the house.

The next thing I knew, it was Christmas morning. I looked out the window and watched the sun rise over the top of the trees. Once the sun was up, I ran into Mama and Daddy's room and jumped in the middle of the bed. One of Mama's rules was no presents until the sun was up. They both groaned and mumbled something about coffee. I kept jumping up and down until they got out of bed.

"Calm down, Christie Ann. Your presents aren't going anywhere," Mama said.

I grabbed Daddy's arm and began to drag him down the hall.

I walked into the sitting room and saw the dollhouse sitting in front of the tree. I squealed and ran over and crouched down in front of it. There was a little family inside: a mama, a daddy, a little girl, and a boy. It was three stories high, and each room was furnished with little couches and chairs. The kitchen even had pots and pans! I jumped up and hugged Mama and Daddy.

My mother didn't believe in lying to children, so I knew the gifts were from them and not Santa Claus. Mama and Daddy argued about it every year, but as Mama said, the cat was already out of the bag, so it was too late to try to convince me there was a Santa Claus or an Easter Bunny. I was so happy about my dollhouse. I didn't even ask about the Swiss Army knife or the fire truck. When Mama went into the kitchen to put the cinnamon rolls Ernestine had made into the oven, Daddy handed me a Swiss Army knife wrapped in some tissue paper. I hugged him hard and went and hid it in my room.

The rest of my presents were clothes and books. I played with the dollhouse until it was time to get dressed to go to my grandparents' house. If Christmas at my dad's mom flew by, Christmas at my mom's parents took forever. We went to church first and then over to their house for lunch. Daddy always skipped church and just met us at their house to eat. We had to dress up, and the children had to eat in the kitchen, but we couldn't talk. The adults ate in the dining room and talked about the "issues" of the day. As far as I could tell, the women gossiped and the men just sat there. Then they would have coffee and dessert, then the women would clean up, and finally, we would open gifts.

My grandparents bought me a sweater every year. I'm not sure where my grandmother shopped, but the colors of the sweaters she bought were not known in nature. This year, it was a blue sweater with sparkles woven into the fabric. I hated it, but I knew Mama would make me wear it the next time I saw my grandparents. Finally, after all the presents were opened, we would head home. My mother would always say, "Well, that was nice," and my dad would grunt. Christmas was over.

Over the next few weeks, I would come home each day and go straight to my room to play with my dollhouse. In the house I created, the mother was in charge and had a career, while the daddy stayed home and took care of the kids. One afternoon as I was playing, the wall between the kitchen and dining room started leaning. I pushed on it, and it fell over. I yelled for Mama, and she came running into my room.

"What on earth are you yelling about?"

"My wall just fell down."

Mama came over and looked at it. "I was afraid this was going to happen. Your daddy was deep in the Crown Royal when he was putting it together. There were a lot of screws left over, but he said they were just extras."

That night, I met Daddy at the door when he got home from work and told him what happened. He said he would look at it after dinner, but he fell asleep in his recliner and didn't look at it. I bugged him every day for a week, but he never got around to it. Every time I tried to play with it, a different wall would fall over. Daddy told me to grab some duct tape out of the shed and tape the walls back up. Now instead of a beautiful home, I had something that looked like Old Leroy's junk truck. It was ugly, and I stopped playing with it. The next time I saw it was at my grandmother's yard sale.

I later found out Daddy couldn't remember where he had put the extra screws. Mama said he ripped the shed apart but could never find them. Later, when I was a teenager, I opened the junk drawer in the kitchen to find the Scotch tape, and at the bottom of the drawer was a little bag full of screws. I took them out and put them in my dresser drawer.

Chapter Eight

Soon, school was over, and it was summertime again, which meant Jimmy time. Mrs. Jefferson recommended I skip a grade, but Daddy said no. I was happy to stay with the same group of kids I went to kindergarten and first and second grade with. They didn't call me a baby anymore, and they let me play with them at recess and eat with them at lunch, so I was happy. Of course, Mama bragged to everyone that the teacher wanted me to skip a grade. No wonder my cousins were so mean to me. I would get tired of hearing about how smart I was too.

Jimmy arrived at the beginning of June. He was staying for a month. I had recently visited my cousin Wayne in Texas, and he had a tree house. It was basically a few boards nailed together to make a floor, and then those boards were nailed to a tree limb, but it was fun to sit up high and watch everyone down below. People forgot we were up there, so we watched Wayne's sister making out with the boy next door and saw Mama sneaking a cigarette and my dad taking a couple shots of whiskey.

I decided building a tree house was going to be mine and Jimmy's summer project. We had recently had our old porch rebuilt, and the wood that the carpenters ripped up was behind the shed. I told Jimmy my idea, and he was all in, that is until he picked up one of the boards and there were bugs stuck to it. He screamed and threw the board down.

"You have got to stop screaming like a little girl," I said. "It's embarrassing."

"We don't have snakes and bugs in Houston. It's all concrete. I don't like things that bite."

"Those aren't even real bugs. They're roly polys. Good lord."

I reached down and grabbed a couple of boards and put them in the wheelbarrow. We had chosen a tree about a hundred yards from our house, right on the edge of the woods. I grabbed Daddy's hammer and some nails out of the coffee can on his workbench, and we walked out to the tree. I wanted my tree house to look like a real house. I started nailing boards on the tree to use as steps. When I was about four steps from the branch where we were going to put the floor, I yelled down for Jimmy to start climbing up. He made it to the second rung and froze.

"Christie. Christie!"

"What?"

"I'm scared," Jimmy said.

"Jimmy, I swear you act more like a girl every time I see you. Just climb up and don't look down."

He climbed up one more step and stopped.

"I can't do it. Can we build a playhouse on the ground instead of a tree house?"

"Jimmy, the whole point of having a tree house is so you can spy on people. If you have a playhouse on the ground, there's nowhere to hide. People can see you, and then they won't talk or do secret things. A playhouse won't be any fun!"

"Well, I'm not climbing up that tree, so you better figure something else out."

I climbed down the tree, threw the hammer on the ground, and stalked off. Jimmy was acting like a sissy, and I couldn't take it anymore. I was going to build a tree house even if I had to do it myself. I told Jimmy to go home, and I went into the house, slamming the door behind me. I went in my room, took out a piece of my drawing paper, and began to draw plans for my tree house. I would need a way to get the boards up to the limb, but I thought I could use a rope tied to a cardboard box. I went out to Daddy's shed and started digging around.

I found rope and a wooden box that was lightweight. It was made of slats, so I stuck the rope through two of the slats and made a knot. I picked it up and carried it out to the tree where I had left the boards. I threw one end of the rope over a limb and grabbed it. I threw a board in the box and began to climb the rungs I had nailed in earlier, pulling the box at the same time. When I was about halfway up the tree, the box began to swing back and forth, and I couldn't control it. I tried to hold onto the rope and keep climbing, but my foot missed the next rung and I fell. When I hit the ground, it knocked the wind out of me. I looked down and saw my arm was twisted at a very strange angle. I could see what looked like bone sticking out near my elbow.

I sat up, used my good arm to pull myself up on my knees, stood up, and walked in the back door, yelling for Ernestine. She came running in from the living room. "Lord, child, you scared me to death. What's the matter?" She saw me holding my arm and ran over to look at it. "Oh lord, oh lord." She took off running down the hall to the sitting room. I could hear her yelling for my mother. Mama came into the hall and said, "Good lord, Ernestine, why all the racket?" Ernestine grabbed her upper arm and pulled her into the kitchen. Mama saw my arm and fainted dead away. Ernestine bent down to take care of mama while I walked slowly to the telephone and called Dr. Turnley's office. I told the nurse who answered what had happened, and she said she would send the doctor right over. I sat down at the kitchen table to wait.

Ernestine was waving, smelling salts under Mama's nose. She finally came to, saw me again, and ran to the bathroom to throw up. My mother is not what you would call good in a crisis. About that time, there was a knock at the door. I got up and went to open it. Dr. Turnley stood there with his black doctor's bag.

"Well, I heard you had a pretty bad fall. Break something?"

"Yes, sir."

I held my arm out for him to look at.

"Well, I say you did. Let me come in and look."

He walked into the kitchen and told me to sit down on one of the breakfast table chairs. He picked up my arm and looked at the bone poking through the skin.

"Well, the good news is, it's a clean break. I will set it and sew up the hole where the bone went through. We need to go to my office. Where's your mama so I can tell her?"

About that time, Ernestine came running into the living room, yelling that we needed to call Dr. Turnley. She ran right past him.

"Ernestine. ERNESTINE!" Dr. Turnley yelled.

Ernestine stopped dead in her tracks and turned back to look at me and Dr. Turnley. He told her my arm was broken, and he was going to take me to his office to set it. He told her to have Mama pick me up in an hour. He helped me up and led me out to his car. My arm was hurting bad, but I didn't say anything. Mama had always told me not to complain. Southern women were supposed to be soft inside with a hard shell on the outside. I must have fallen asleep in his car because before I knew it, we were at his office.

He came around to my side of the car and opened the door. He gently took me by my good arm and led me into the clinic. Nurse Kathy, whom I had known since I was born, fussed over me and took me into an exam room. She gave me a little white pill to put under my tongue and told me to lay back. The pill was very bitter. I felt my eyes getting heavy, and before I knew it, I heard Daddy talking to Dr. Turnley. I opened my eyes and said, "Daddy?" He walked over to the table and started brushing my hair off my face. "You okay, Sunshine?"

"I fell," I said.

"I know you did," he said. "You broke your arm. Why on earth where you climbing a tree with wood in a box?"

"I wanted to build a tree house. Jimmy was too scared to help me take the wood up the tree, so I tried to pull it up in the box. I missed a step and fell. My arm hurts. Where's Mama?"

"She's at home making you some chicken and dumplings and chocolate pie."

The only two things my mother cooked well were chicken and dumplings and chocolate pie, which was great for me because those were two of my favorite things. I knew Mama wouldn't be at the clinic when I woke up. Anything to do with blood or body functions put her over the edge. She refused to go to the doctor. She believed in herbal tonics that Ernestine made for her. She never ate, and she smoked every chance she got, but basically, she was in pretty good shape.

Once Dr. Turnley was finished, Daddy picked me up and carried me out to the truck and laid me down on the seat. I fell asleep again on the way home. I woke up when the truck stopped. I told Daddy I could walk in by myself. When I walked through the screen door into the house, Mama came running into the living room, grabbed me, and started hugging and kissing me all at the same time. She finally stood up, straightened her skirt, and told me I could eat off a TV tray in the living room. I knew it must be bad if Mama was letting me eat off a TV tray. Daddy was the only one allowed to do that. I sat down, and Mama brought in a tray full of food. She sat down and started to try to feed me.

"Mother, I can do it myself. I broke my left arm, not the one I use."

"Okay. Well, I'm right here if you need me."

She continued to sit by me on the sofa and watch every bite I took. After about four bites, I started to get tired again, so I asked Mama if I could go to my room and lay down. She said sure and followed me into my bedroom. She helped me put on my pajama pants and my Yankees baseball shirt. My daddy was a big Mickey Mantle fan, and because of that, I loved the New York Yankees. People in the town we lived in couldn't understand why my parents would allow me wear a T-shirt that said Yankees on it, but Daddy said not to worry about them. He said it gave them something to talk about. Mama put a pillow under my arm and kissed my forehead. If I had known breaking my arm would make Mama this nice, I would have done it a long time ago. I fell asleep.

The next morning, I woke up stiff and in pain. I yelled for Daddy, and Mama came running into the room instead. She was holding a glass of water and a little blue pill. I told her I didn't want to take it because it made my head feel fuzzy. She said feeling a little fuzzy was okay while my arm healed. She told me she had made my favorite pecan, brown sugar pancakes. My mother did not know how to make pancakes. They were usually burned on the outside and raw in the middle. I told her I wasn't hungry. She told me she would keep them warm for me. She helped me to the bathroom, but I made her wait outside.

"Honey, how are you going to wipe properly?"

"I have one good arm, Mother."

She asked me if I wanted her to help me with my bath. I asked her where Ernestine was. My mother had never bathed me, even when I was little. Ernestine was the only person who could see me without clothes on. Mama let out a big sigh and yelled for Ernestine.

I sat down on the side of the bathtub and waited. Ernestine came into the bathroom and shut the door. She pulled a bacon biscuit out of her apron pocket and handed it to me. Ernestine knew me like a book. I gobbled it down and drank some water from the faucet. Ernestine had a roll of cling wrap, and she wound it around my cast so it wouldn't get wet. She helped me take off my clothes and put some bubbles in the bath. I climbed in and sat down. It felt wonderful. She folded up a towel and told me to lay back. She put some Epsom salts in the water and told me to just soak the soreness away and to holler if I needed anything.

I lay back on the towel and closed my eyes. A little while later, I jerked awake and realized I was pruney and the water was cold. I yelled for Ernestine. The door opened, and Mama walked in. I tried to cover myself with the towel, but she came over and took my good arm and pulled me to a standing position. She started drying me off, and I grabbed the towel and told her I could do it myself. She looked at me for a long moment, and then Ernestine came flying into the bathroom.

"Oh, Mrs. Cook, I didn't know you was in here. I'll get back to the ironing."

"No, Ernestine. Go ahead. She doesn't want me."

I was still standing in the tub with the towel covering me. Mama walked out, and Ernestine started rubbing my hair—hard. I yelled, "Ow!" She slowed down and told me that I had hurt Mama's feelings. I told her I didn't think Mama had feelings. Ernestine whirled me around and popped me on my naked butt. "You don't talk like that about yo mama. She loves you in her own way, and she would give her life just to keep you from suffering even one minute of pain." I didn't believe that, but I ducked my head and said, "Sorry." Ernestine picked me up out of the tub and put me on the rug on the bathroom floor. She helped me put on some clothes, brushed my hair, and helped me walk down the hall to my bedroom. I climbed into the bed and laid back on my pillow. I was already half asleep. Ernestine kissed me and began to walk out.

"Ernestine?"

"What, child?"

"Why doesn't Mama take care of me like you do?"

Ernestine never turned around. "Because she don't know how."

The next day, I was lying on the porch swing with a pillow behind my head and my bad arm laying across my stomach reading *Mad Magazine* when Jimmy sidled up to the porch.

"How you doing?" he asked.

"I'm good," I said.

"I'm real sorry about your arm. I should have been able to catch you."

I didn't think Jimmy could catch a cold, much less me.

"It's all right. I shouldn't have tried to do it myself."

"Well, we could try again. I promise I won't get scared this time."

"Jimmy, my arm is broken. I can't climb a tree."

Jimmy found a rock in the dirt and kicked it. He stood there with his hands in his pockets, staring at the ground.

"Do you want to play Monopoly," I asked.

He brightened up and said, "Sure."

I sent him into the house to get the game, and we set it up on the floor of the porch. I beat him, but we had fun. We spent the rest of his visit at his grandparents' house playing board games and card games. It was a lazy summer but enjoyable. Before I knew it, Jimmy left to go back to Houston. My cast came off the week before school started. My wrist wasn't aligned correctly with the rest of my arm, but it didn't look too bad.

Chapter Nine

That fall, I started third grade at Olla Elementary. One of the Robbins twins, I could never tell them apart, told me there was no Santa Clause or Easter Bunny. I told him I had known that since I was three. I also told him, I think he was the twin named Robert, that I was not surprised with his limited intellect that it took him eight years to figure it out. Not understanding any of those words, he told me I was weird and ran off.

Each year in September, the fair came to Olla. Daddy and I always went. Mama didn't like the carnival workers and the dust that wafted up from the ground as you walked, so she stayed home. I never said anything, but Daddy and I had more fun without Mama. He pretty much let me do whatever I wanted within reason, so, of course, he was my favorite. We arrived at the fair around five o'clock and made our first stop at the corn dog and lemonade stand. I loved corn dogs, but Mama would never buy them from the Piggly Wiggly, so I always looked forward to having one at the fair. Next, we went and bought our tickets. Five dollars bought fifty tickets, and the rides were two tickets each, so that meant I could ride twenty-five times. My favorite rides were the Tilt-A-Whirl and the Ferris wheel. Most of the tickets were used for those two rides.

After riding for an hour or so, we walked over to the cotton candy truck. While we were standing in line waiting our turn, we heard yelling and a sound like someone was kicking something hard. There was a crowd gathered around where the noise was coming from, and Daddy and I went over to look. Someone pushed me to the front of the circle, and I lost Daddy's hand. I saw a man stomping on the head of a little black boy. The little boy was screaming and crying, and the man just kept stomping on his head with his cowboy boots. Nobody did anything to stop him. About that time, Sheriff Franklin pushed through the crowd and grabbed the man's arms from behind. He threw him to the ground and handcuffed him. He saw Daddy in the crowd and told him to go call the hospital for an ambulance. Mr. Thompson, who went to our church, told Daddy he would watch me.

I looked at the little boy, and he had blood all over his face, and he wasn't moving. Someone in the crowd said, "What happened?" I heard another person say, "That little nigger boy was running and knocked James's daughter down." I couldn't believe what I had just witnessed and all because he knocked a little girl down. I'm sure he didn't mean to. Daddy walked up behind me and put his hands on my shoulders. The paramedics arrived, but there was nothing they could do. The little boy was dead.

Daddy said, "Let's go."

We walked back to the truck holding hands. I looked up at Daddy and could see tears falling down his cheeks. I asked him what was wrong. He said the little boy's name was Henry, and he was Ernestine's nephew's son. He said we should probably go on over to Ernestine's house and see if there was anything we could do. We drove over to the quarters where all the black people lived. When we drove into the yard, all the lights in the house were on, and there were cars and trucks parked everywhere. We got out of the truck and walked up the porch steps. Ernestine's husband, Clyde, was standing on the porch with three other men. He shook Daddy's hand and mussed my hair. "How you doing, squirt?" Mr. Clyde always called me squirt.

"I heard you saw it happen," Mr. Clyde said to Daddy.

"We walked up about the same time the sheriff got there," Daddy said.

"Heard you went and called for the ambulance?"

"I did."

"Well, we appreciate it, Mr. Nick. You always been good to this family. You know there's gonna be a trial? They arrested the man who did it. They might call you to tell what you saw happen. People think you on our side, it could cause trouble for you."

"You let me handle that, Clyde."

"Yes, sir."

"Is Ernestine okay?" Daddy asked.

"She's managing. You know she thought of Henry as another son. Eight years old and stomped to death for accidentally knocking over a little white girl. It's never gonna get any better, is it, Mr. Nick?"

"We can't think that way, Clyde. We have to keep up the good fight."

"Yes, sir."

I pulled on Mr. Clyde's shirt and asked if I could go see Ernestine. He told me she was in the front room with her sisters. I walked in and followed the sound of voices talking. I stood at the door of the room where Ernestine and her family were. Ernestine's sister, Carla, saw me, came over, and hugged me. She took my hand and led me to Ernestine. I stood in front of her with my head hung. She grabbed me by the chin and pulled my head up to look at me. She had been crying. She asked me why I was hanging my head. I told her I was so ashamed that a white man had killed Henry. She grabbed me, pulled me onto her lap, and started rocking me.

I was too big to be sitting on her lap, but I felt safe there. Ernestine always smelled like jasmine and chocolate chip cookies. She told me it wasn't my fault that white man killed Henry and not to ever take that guilt on myself. She said if the man didn't get punished in this world, he certainly would in the next. I don't remember how long I sat on her lap, but the next thing I knew, Daddy was waking me up to go home. We said goodbye to everyone and got in the truck. I was shivering and couldn't stop. Daddy reached behind the seat and grabbed his camouflage hunting jacket for me to put on. Even with the jacket, I continued to shake.

Mama was waiting up for us. I was still shivering, so she took me to my room and helped me put on my flannel pajamas from the winter before. They were too short, but I didn't care. She asked me if I wanted to talk about it, and I said no; then I burst into tears. I asked her to stay with me until I fell asleep. She said she would sit in the rocker by my bed. I finally fell asleep. When I woke up as dawn was coming through the windows, Mama was still sitting in the rocker.

The man who killed Henry was named James Davis. He was a bad man and had been in jail before for beating his wife. There was a trial like Mr. Clyde said, and Daddy had to testify. The Davis man was found guilty and was sentenced to three years in prison. Daddy was mad about the time he had to serve. He said he should have been sent to prison for the rest of his life. One of the man's brothers came to Daddy's work with two of his friends. They were going to hurt Daddy, but Daddy took his pistol out of his desk drawer and told them he couldn't kill all three of them at once, but he would make damn sure he got at least one of them. They left, and we didn't hear from them again.

Many years later when I was a teenager, I saw the Davis man in the Five and Dime. I knew who he was because I had seen his picture in the newspaper when the trial was going on. He hadn't changed much. He looked at me, smirked, and said, "You're that nigger lover's daughter." I looked him right in the eye and said, "Yes, sir, I am." Then I turned around and walked out of the store without buying the thread Mama wanted. When I got home, I told her they didn't have the color she needed. I never told anyone about my interaction with that man, but I felt so much hate toward him; I wanted to do something to hurt him as bad as he had hurt Henry.

Chapter Ten

The school year ended, and the entire summer lay before me. Jimmy was going to California to spend the summer with his dad, so I had no one to play with. I spent a few weeks with my mama's parents, and me, Mama, and Daddy took a vacation to Dogpatch in Arkansas. It was fun even though Mama took our own sheets and towels. Ernestine was still working for us, but she was getting older and moved slower. Her daughter Annette came with her quite a bit and started taking over some of the cooking and cleaning. I loved Annette, but she wasn't Ernestine. She didn't hug me or ask how my day went. She didn't sit at the kitchen table and listen to all my problems. Ernestine spent a lot of time in the rocker in the kitchen, telling Annette what to do and how to do it. Summer ended, and I started fourth grade. I was excited about fourth grade because there was a writing contest for fourth and fifth graders, and the grand prize was ten dollars.

I had my eye on a Schwinn bike at the hardware store. Daddy said if I saved half the money, he would pay for the other half. The bike was $49.95. I had saved fifteen dollars from birthdays and helping my grandma with her rummage sale. If I could win the writing contest, I would have enough for my half of the bike. I had no doubt I would win the contest. I had been writing stories since I was five, and all my teachers told me how talented I was.

I decided to write about the civil rights movement. The civil rights movement had been going on for years, but things had been bad for black people long before then. There was a little black boy named Emmett Till who had been murdered by some white men in

1955. They killed him because one of their wives said Emmett whistled at her. She came out sixty years later and said she had lied. Then there were the three civil rights workers who were also murdered because they were trying to help black people register to vote. Their car was found in a mud pit on a farm in Mississippi.

I worked on my story for two weeks. I let Ernestine read it, and she said it should be published in *Life* magazine. I turned it into the office and waited to receive my prize. Several days later, Mr. Horton sent a note to my teacher asking her to send me to the office. I walked slowly down the hall trying to think of what I had done. I told the Robbins twins they were morons, but I said that all the time. I arrived at the office, and Mr. Horton told me to come in. He shut the door. Mama was there. I started sweating. I could tell by the look on Mama's face she was mad. Mr. Horton told me that he couldn't submit my story in the writing contest. He said I was ahead of my time and that people didn't want to read about little boys being murdered or people being lynched. He said people wanted to read about kittens and puppies. He said he was going to withdraw my story from the contest, but I could try again next year. Mama told me to go get my things from my classroom that I was leaving for the day.

I was confused. If people didn't talk about all the bad things happening in the world, how were they ever going to get any better? Ernestine's daughter Felicia was in Mississippi working hard so black people could have equal rights. Ernestine bragged about her all the time. I thought she was very brave. She had gone to Tuscaloosa College, which was a college for black people. She was supersmart.

My heart felt heavy. All the people who had given their lives, who had been beaten, and abused and for what? Nothing was changing. I realized at that moment that no matter how hard people like Felicia worked, you can't change ignorance.

We went by Daddy's office on the way home. I just sat in the car. I didn't want to see or talk to anyone. Daddy came out and opened the car door. He squatted down and asked me how I was doing. "Not good, Daddy."

He said, "I know, Sunshine. I don't know if it will help, but your Mama and I believe you would have won that contest, so we're going to go ahead and get you that bike."

I thanked him, but it felt like a hollow victory. Me and Mama went home, and I went straight to my room and laid down on the bed. Mama tried to get me to come eat supper, but I wasn't hungry. I lay awake most of the night.

Chapter Eleven

Time rocked on like it always does, but I felt different. Before the writing contest incident, I truly believed things would get better, that black and white people would be equal, and that all the fighting and killing would stop. After the president was assassinated and Henry was murdered, I lost hope. Chaney, Goodman, and Schwerner gave their lives for a cause they believed in and what good did it do. Children were being hung by ropes from trees just because they were black. I was raised to believe in God and that if you prayed to him and were a good person, good things would happen to you. That didn't make sense. What about all the people who were doing good things and were being killed? Where was God when they cried out for him begging for their lives? Where was God when Henry was being stomped to death?

Brown v. the Board of Education was a landmark case that said blacks and whites had to go to school together. Since Louisiana was behind in everything else, we didn't have our first black student until 1966. Her name was Viola Mosley, and she dressed better than most of the hillbilly kids I went to school with. She was nice and quiet, and I wanted her to be my friend. On her first day, I asked her if she wanted to sit with me at lunch. She told me that wasn't a good idea. She said she was going to eat lunch in the principal's office. I said, "Well, do you want to play at recess?" She said she wasn't going out for recess. I was perplexed.

After school that day when I was having my cookies and milk, I told Ernestine about it. She was quiet for a long time. "Ms. Christie, that little girl playing with you could get you both hurt or worse. You need to leave it alone."

"But, Ernestine, if we don't get to be friends with each other, how will things get any better?"

She had been cleaning the oven. She turned around and sat at the table with me. "Hon, I don't think it will get better. Not in my lifetime anyway."

"Daddy says we have to keep fighting the good fight," I replied.

Ernestine said, "I'm tired, child. I've lost too much and for what so my people can vote. Vote for who? White people who don't care what we have to say and don't want us to get an education or even eat with them? I'm starting to think the price is just too high." She stood back up and went out on the porch. I didn't know what to think. Ernestine had always been steadfast in her fight for equal rights. If she was giving up, where did that leave me?

Ernestine started coming to our house less and less. Annette was handling all the housework and cooking, but she wasn't very interested in me. She would have a snack waiting for me after school, but it was usually vanilla wafers or graham crackers with a glass of milk. No more homemade cookies. Annette was saving her money to move to Chicago. She said things were different for black people in the North. She said blacks and whites went to school together and everybody got along. She said there were good jobs for black people there. Her cousin was working in a toy factory up North, and she made as much in one week as Annette made in a whole month. Annette told me black people weren't beat or hung in trees. She said if she worked for us six more months, she would have enough money to go. I asked her who would take care of me when she left, and she said, "Your mama will."

I didn't like the sound of that. Mama was still making me go to Ms. Parker's house for etiquette lessons, but the visits had become sporadic. One day when Mama was picking me up, I heard Ms. Parker tell her she was wasting her time on me. She told Mama I didn't have an ounce of grace in my body, and I was the most stubborn child she had ever worked with. She said it was simple, I didn't want to learn how to become a lady, so I refused to try to learn what she was teaching me. After that conversation, Mama didn't make me go as much.

We were halfway through fourth grade, and I was glad we were finally reading chapter books. I had read most of the ones on the list Ms. Jackson gave us, but we were currently reading Tom Sawyer, and I thought it was a great book. I especially liked Huck Finn and could relate to him. One afternoon, I came home from school and Mama was sitting on the porch swing with a suitcase beside her. Daddy was sitting in the rocking chair, and his face was blood red.

"What's going on?" I asked.

"Your mother has decided to leave us and move to New Orleans."

"What? Why?" I asked.

Mama told me to come sit next to her, but I went and stood by Daddy. She cleared her throat and said she just needed something new. She didn't feel like she was growing as a person, and she felt like she was suffocating. She said she had always been somebody's daughter or wife or mother, and she just wanted to be herself for a while. I just stared at her.

"Are you going to be gone forever?"

"Of course not. I will be back to visit, and you can come visit me once I get settled."

Daddy said under his breath, "Over my dead body."

Mama looked at Daddy a second too long, and then she looked back at me. She told me she loved me and Daddy, and it wasn't our fault she was leaving. She just wanted to be by herself for a while. She said she wanted to be where things were happening. She said nothing new and exciting ever happened in Olla. She told me to be good for Daddy and Annette, and she would come visit soon. She asked if she could have a hug and a kiss, but I refused to leave Daddy's side. She picked up her suitcase, walked out to our old station wagon, climbed in, and drove off.

I looked at Daddy, and he said, "Well, I guess that's that. You want to go to the Burger Barn for supper?" So we went.

I felt bad because I didn't really miss Mama. I felt like she was always disappointed in me and would have liked to have a different little girl—a little girl who wore pink and played with Barbies and read *Wuthering Heights*. I wasn't that girl. Daddy and I did fine until Annette moved to Chicago. After she left, the house wasn't being cleaned, and we were both tired of the Burger Barn. Sometimes, I wore a T-shirt two or three times before Daddy would remember to do a load of laundry. I received letters from Mama, but I just put them in my drawer unread.

Daddy hired and fired several women who were supposed to cook, clean, and take care of me. When Mama was living with us, Daddy would have two or three beers on the weekend. Now he was drinking every day. I missed Ernestine, but she was too old to take care of me anymore. I basically started taking care of myself. I figured out how to do laundry and cook some basic things like spaghetti and fried bologna. I tried to keep the house clean, but my heart wasn't really in it. I did sweep and mop at least once a week, but I hated dusting and refused to clean bathrooms.

Fourth grade ended, and it was summertime again. Jimmy didn't come visit his grandparents. They felt they were too old to watch him properly, so I didn't see him that year. We wrote letters back and forth a few times and then lost touch. Why write a letter when there was nothing new to say?

I went to spend a week with my cousins Dan and Deann, my aunt Dottie, and my uncle Danny. Daddy had to go out of town on business, and he said I was too young to stay by myself, so I went to their house. If I thought our house was dirty and disorganized, Aunt Dottie took it to a whole new level. One morning, I woke up and Aunt Dottie was reading and drinking coffee. Everyone else was still asleep, so I pulled a box of cereal out of the cabinet. I couldn't find a clean bowl.

"Aunt Dottie, are there clean bowls somewhere?"

"Probably not," she said.

"Well, what am I supposed to eat my cereal out of?"

"Is there a glass clean?"

I looked in the cabinet. "Yes, ma'am."

"Use that and a teaspoon."

I thought that was the coolest idea I had ever heard.

Aunt Dottie taught me all about scary books and movies. She gave me my first horror story, *The Bad Seed.* I thought the book explained a lot about some of the kids I went to school with. Later, she introduced me to Stephen King, who is still my favorite. Aunt Dottie and Ernestine were the only two people I had told about my dream of becoming a writer. Aunt Dottie was very supportive and would give me constructive criticism when she read my stories. She taught me how to make a story flow and that you need to mix humor and drama in equal measures. I lost her to cancer when I was twenty-seven. I still miss her every day.

There was a big mound behind Dan and Deann's house, and my cousin Dan had convinced us it was an old Indian burial ground. We did find some arrowheads close to the mound, but I've always wondered if Dan bought them at the flea market and hid them for us to find. He told us the area around the mound was haunted.

It was summer in Louisiana, so it was hot and there were mosquitoes everywhere. Everyone walked around with flyswatters in their hands, and everyone slept with the windows open with no screens. You slept under a sheet, and when you would wake in the morning, the sheet and your entire body would be wet with sweat. One night, Dan had a friend over. His name was Clay, and I had a huge crush on him. He and Dan played in the band at their church, and they were best friends. That night, Deann and I lay awake, giggling and talking about people we knew. Finally, about 11:30 p.m. I dosed off only to be startled awake by something that looked like it was wearing an Indian headdress standing over my side of the bed. I had my flyswatter in my hand, so I screamed and poked where I thought the eye might be. Somebody howled and fell back into the wall. The lights in the hall came on, and my aunt Dottie came screaming down the hall with an empty beer bottle in her hand.

I realized the voice coming from the Indian getup was my cousin Dan, and he was crying. He kept saying, "You poked me in the eye. You poked me in the eye!" Aunt Dottie flipped on the bedroom light and grabbed Dan by his make-believe Indian headdress that was made of sticks tied together with twine and crow's feathers. He was screaming about me poking him in the eye with the flyswatter (I used the end you hold), and she was yelling about those nasty crow feathers being brought into her house. She pulled him by the sticks that were embedded in his hair out the back door and into the yard. Then she came back in the house breathing hard, telling us all to lay down and shut up or she was going to start "whuppin' some ass."

Clay went outside to check on Dan, and Deann and I started laughing and couldn't stop. So much for the haunted burial ground.

When Daddy came home from his trip, he told me that he hadn't really been away on business. He had been to New Orleans to see Mama and see if they could work something out. He said she didn't want to move back to Olla because it was too small, and there was too much family living there. Daddy didn't want to live in New Orleans, so they settled on Houston. He said Mama was in Houston, looking for a place for us to live, and we were going to clean up our house and put it up for sale. I went on a hunger strike and refused to speak to Daddy. On the third day when I still wouldn't talk or eat, he called Ernestine. Ernestine was half blind, and in a wheelchair, but she came.

I heard her wheelchair rolling down the hall toward my room, and I got up and opened the door. She looked so frail. She was wearing thick glasses and a dress with a sweater wrapped around her even though it was a hundred degrees outside. I burst into tears. She held out her arms.

"Oh, sweet child."

I went to my knees so I could put my arms around Ernestine's waist. I cried until there were no tears left. Ernestine had been my touchstone since I was born. She kept all my secrets, knew all my moods, and loved me I believed more than anyone else I knew. She never tried to change me. She just loved the person I was, and she loved me with all she had. Even though I didn't see her every day, I knew she wasn't far away. If I move to Texas, I may never see her again, and we both knew that. We sat in the hall until the sun went down and the house was dark.

Chapter Twelve

Two weeks later, Daddy and I packed up as much as we could in the back of his truck and my uncle's trailer and headed for Houston. I was a little excited because the house Mama found for us was two streets over from Jimmy's house. I know she thought that would make the move easier for me, but I was still mad at her. I had to leave my school where I finally had friends, my grandparents, my cousins, my aunts, my uncles, and all the people in our little town who knew me, but what broke my heart the most was leaving Ernestine. The night she came to the house to help Daddy end my hunger strike, her husband, Mr. Clyde, told Daddy she didn't have much time left. I was terrified she was going to die, and I wouldn't be there. I knew about the Grim Reaper. Aunt Dottie had told me all about him. I believed if I could be there when he came for Ernestine, I could point the big cross at him that we kept on the wall in the sitting room, and he would disappear and leave Ernestine to live another day. But how could I protect her if I wasn't there?

We moved into the new house in Houston the last week of July, and I hated it. It was only one story, and it was in a neighborhood with other houses. There were no woods, or creek, or cool hiding places like we had at our old house. The front door didn't stick, and it didn't have screen doors or a porch. Mama and Daddy were acting like lovebirds, and it made me sick. I thought Daddy had better sense than that. Mama was a "career woman." She worked at a doctor's office. I was about to go into the fifth grade, and I convinced Mama and Daddy that even though I was only nine years old, I was extremely mature for my age, and I could be trusted to stay alone after school. I finally wore them down by promising to call Mama every two hours and agreeing not to leave the house or let anyone except Jimmy or his mama in.

The first couple of weeks, Mama was strict about the two-hour phone call rule, but after that she didn't push it too much. She knew I was smart enough not to let a stranger in the house or get in the car with one. I heard her and Daddy joking one time that if someone took me, it would be like the book *The Ransom of Red Chief.* I called the library and asked the librarian what the book was about. She told me it was about a little boy who was so bossy that when he was kidnapped, the men who took him called his parents and said they would pay them to take him back. They couldn't handle him. It didn't hurt my feelings because I prided myself on being difficult, but I decided to keep that piece of information in my back pocket in case I needed it later.

One afternoon, I got bored watching soap operas and decided to ride my bike around the block. Mama and Daddy would never know. When I got to the end of the street, I saw a baseball diamond. There were about twelve boys and one girl playing baseball. I felt my heart speed up. I had been playing baseball with my cousins my entire life. I loved baseball. Me and Daddy listened to the Yankees games on the radio every Saturday. I raced back home and grabbed my mitt. For three days, I sat on the outside of the fence behind home plate, watching them play. They completely ignored me. The girl was the pitcher, and she was good. They called her Tater Tot. Finally, at the end of the game on the third day, she walked over to me and said, "Hey, kid. You any good?" I stuttered out a "yeah." She told me to come back the next day and fill in for their first baseman who was out with the chicken pox. I yelled thanks over my shoulder and raced home to start practicing. Maybe Houston wouldn't be so bad after all.

I started playing with the team the next day, and I must have been pretty good because when their regular first baseman came back, they put him in the outfield. I was the youngest member on the team. Most of the kids were eleven or twelve. When school started, we still played. The girl who had initially invited me to be on the team was Kelli Elliott. She was eleven but only one grade ahead of me. She didn't acknowledge me at school, but one time I was in the bathroom and a seventh grader pushed me when she walked to the sink to wash her hands. Kelli jumped in front of me and said something to the girl in a low, mean voice. I don't know what she said, but that girl never bothered me again.

Jimmy and I hung around together, along with a Chinese girl named Chi. We were the smart, geeky kids, but unlike Jimmy and Chi, I was good at sports. I tried out and made the sixth-grade softball team. I was only nine and in the fifth grade, but the PE coach liked me, and she let me act as the bat girl / scorekeeper. Sometimes if we were way ahead in the game, the coach would let me play the last inning. I was making good grades, and even though I missed Olla and my family, Houston wasn't too bad. I called Ernestine every Saturday morning, but the conversations became shorter and shorter. She was fading, but I just refused to see it. Mama tried to talk to me about Ernestine once, and I told her Ernestine was more of a mother to me than she would ever be. She never brought it up again.

Chapter Thirteen

In January of that school year, right after I turned ten, Daddy woke me up in the middle of the night.

"Daddy, what's wrong? What time is it?"

"It's two thirty in the morning. Baby, it's Ernestine."

I started screaming, "No, no," and ran into the kitchen. I grabbed the telephone and began to dial Ernestine's phone number. Daddy took the phone out of my hand and gently hung it up. "She's gone, baby girl." I slid down the wall to the floor sobbing. It was my fault. I wasn't there when the Grim Reaper came. I wasn't there to scare him away. Daddy picked me up and took me back to my bedroom. He sat on the side of the bed and held me until my wails turned into sobs and then whimpers. I saw Mama standing at my bedroom door, but I didn't want her near me. She was the reason we lived in Houston, and she was the reason I wasn't there to save Ernestine. Daddy packed some clothes for all of us, and we left about four thirty that morning headed for Olla.

We went to my grandparents' house since Ernestine had been hired by them when she was only sixteen to help take care of Mama. We arrived around noon, and the house was full of food and people. I went to the backyard where the swing hung from one of the limbs of the old oak tree. I sat down and started slowly pushing myself back and forth. My grandfather walked over to me and asked me if I wanted a push.

"No thanks, Papaw."

"Did you know Pepper had another litter of puppies?"

Pepper was Papaw's Catahoula Cur. She was a great dog, and I had been begging for one of her puppies for the last three years ever since he started breeding her. Papaw only let her have one litter a year, and the puppies were always sold before they were even born. He said he was going to have her fixed; her time to have puppies was over.

"They're just about ready to be weaned. You want to see 'em?"

I was sad, but I wasn't going to miss a chance to see Pepper's puppies. We walked over to the barn, and there they were. There was a little white male with brown spots on his back and his ears. I squatted down, and he came over and sat down on my foot. I laughed. Papaw squatted down beside me.

"Looks like he's taken a liking to you."

"Doesn't matter. Mama's allergic."

"Do you want him?"

I rubbed the puppy behind the ears, and he leaned into my hand. I wanted him bad, but I knew it wasn't going to happen.

"Mama won't let me."

"You let me worry about your mama. Seems to me she's been getting everything she wants lately—new city, new house, new job—maybe it's time you got something you want for a change."

I looked at my grandfather, and he winked at me. I jumped up and hugged him around the neck almost knocking him over. My grandfather always smelled like pipe tobacco. I loved that smell, and to this day if someone is smoking a pipe, I get a lump in my throat. Everyone I knew said my grandfather was a good man. He worked for the same company for forty years, raised five children, bought and paid for a home, and bought a new car every three years, all without knowing how to read and write. He was one of the smartest men I knew.

He asked me what I was going to name the puppy, and I said, "Lincoln, because Abraham Lincoln freed the slaves, and Ernestine always said Abraham Lincoln was a good man."

Papaw rubbed the puppy on the head and said, "I think Lincoln's a fine name."

I stayed in the barn with the puppy until it was time to go to the funeral. I went in, took a bath, and let my aunt Joyce curl my hair and dress me. I wore a blue dress with little white spots. Ernestine always said I looked pretty in blue. I knew Ernestine loved me no matter what I wore, but I wanted to look pretty for her. I wanted her to be proud of me. I don't remember much about the funeral. I knew it was long. When it was time to go up to the casket, I just couldn't do it. Daddy understood and walked me outside to sit at one of the picnic tables. We didn't say a word, but his presence gave me comfort. Daddy was always there for me and knew my moods better than anyone, except for Ernestine. Then it was over, and everyone came outside to eat.

Mama made me a plate, and I was picking at it when Mr. Clyde, Ernestine's husband, came over and sat down beside me. He handed me a little brown paper bag.

"Ernestine was in and out toward the end, but on one of her good days, she told me to make sure you got this."

I opened the bag and took out the charm bracelet that Ernestine always wore. Her children had given her many different charms. The bracelet Mr. Clyde gave me had a charm of Martin Luther King Jr. There was a tiny replica of *To Kill a Mockingbird*, a cross that I had given her for Christmas one year, and a picture of me when I was a baby. She had taken off some of the other charms and given those to her children and grandchildren, but she left the charms that were important to me. I cried as I fastened it on my wrist. I choked out a thank-you to Mr. Clyde and hugged his neck.

"She loved you something fierce, little girl."

"Yes, sir, I know. Thank you."

I looked down at the bracelet. It was too big, but I knew I would grow into it. I never took it off, and I still wear it to this day.

We left the next morning heading back to Houston with Lincoln in tow. Mama said he was making her eyes water, but she turned around and petted him a couple of times. He was a great puppy and slept most of the way home.

Chapter Fourteen

My fifth-grade year was coming to an end, and I had settled into a routine. I still missed Ernestine desperately, and sometimes when I was alone in my room, I would talk to her. Lincoln helped with the sadness. It's hard to be sad when there's a puppy climbing all over you. I took him everywhere with me. He liked to chase the baseballs we missed when we were playing, and he became the team mascot in pretty short order. I came home at lunch every day and played with him and walked him.

On the way home from Ernestine's funeral, Mama said he had to sleep in the laundry room, and he absolutely could not get on any of the furniture. That lasted about three days until she got sick of him crying at night. He slept at the foot of my bed and pretty much did whatever else he wanted. Daddy wanted to breed him, but Mama said she wasn't going to be responsible for trying to sell puppies, knowing full well I would want to keep them all, so we had him fixed. He got fat, but he was still a happy dog, and he was great for me to bury my head in his fur when I was crying and didn't want anyone to hear.

Before I knew it, summer was back, and it was hot enough to fry eggs on the sidewalk. Jimmy and I tried it one day, and it actually worked. I still played baseball at the neighborhood field, but Jimmy didn't like baseball, so I tried to do some stuff with him too. His dad had sent him a chemistry set, and we decided we were going to try to make some stink bombs and put them in the garbage cans of some of the kids who made fun of us. The chemistry set would never be sold these days. It had potassium nitrate in it for Christ's sake, enough to create an exploding stink bomb. We waited until my parents left for work one day; then we took the chemistry set into the kitchen and started working on the "project." We stole a box of matches from my mom's bedside table, cut the heads off, and put them in a jar. We put in some ammonia, and then we added the potassium nitrate. According to the chemistry set, once someone opened the jar, it would blow the smell right into the face of the person who opened it. We followed the directions but decided we better try it out ourselves before we let it loose on some unsuspecting victim.

According to the directions, we had to wait three days before we opened the jar. Jimmy saw himself as a mad scientist, so he wanted to be the one to open the jar. When the big day finally arrived, we were so excited. We took the jar outside to the carport, and Jimmy began to open it. As soon as oxygen got in between the lid and the inside of the jar, it blew the top right off, taking Jimmy's eyebrows and eyelashes right along with it. If that wasn't bad enough, the stench was horrible. I started gagging, and Jimmy was screaming about his eyelashes and eyebrows. Once I got a good look at him, I started laughing and couldn't stop.

Jimmy was pale anyway, but now that his eyelashes and eyebrows were missing, he looked like an albino I had seen at the fair once. He kept feeling where his eyebrows used to be, and each time he realized they weren't there, he yelled. "It blew my damn eyebrows clean off." Every time he said it, I just laughed harder. We decided to try to get rid of the smell by burying the jar. When my dad got home from work that night, he looked at Jimmy and said, "Did you get a haircut?" That just made me laugh harder. Jimmy packed up his chemistry set and went home. His mama never even noticed his missing eyebrows.

Chapter Fifteen

August came rolling around, and I started sixth grade. It was 1967, and according to Daddy, the "whole damn world had gone crazy." The war in Vietnam was still raging with no end in sight, and in California, hippies were chanting about love and peace. None of those things really affected Texas. Sometimes on the news, there would be a picture of a soldier who lost his life in the war; but after feeling a moment of sadness for his family, I really didn't think about it much. I ran for student council president and lost. I was still the ball girl / scorekeeper for the softball team, but you had to be eleven to be on the roster, and I was only ten. That just gave me another reason to be mad at Mama. If she had let me start kindergarten when I was five like everyone else, I wouldn't always be a year behind. Sixth grade was the year people started pairing up, and Mama sat me down and gave me the "talk." I thought it sounded disgusting and was in no hurry to explore. None of the boys were interested in me anyway. The girls were wearing tight tapered jeans and miniskirts, and I was still wearing blue jeans, denim shirts, and boots.

My dream of being a famous writer was still alive, but the teachers said the things I wrote about were "too mature" for my age. Mama and Daddy were both working, so I spent a lot of time alone. Jimmy and I were growing apart. He had joined the science club and the chess club, and since I didn't care about either of those things and he didn't care about sports, we didn't have much to talk about. Lincoln was my only real friend, and though I talked to him all the time, he never answered back.

In the sixth grade, we changed classes, so I had different teachers for different subjects. I loved my language arts teacher, Mrs. Pugh. Sometimes, I would eat my lunch in her classroom, and we would talk about books and our favorite authors. Mrs. Pugh said she was a bookworm when she was young too. She said she initially wanted to be a writer, but when she went to college, she realized she wasn't good enough to write books, so she decided to teach about them instead. She told me about a program for seventh and eighth graders who were talented writers and asked if she could recommend me for the program. I was thrilled! I might actually find some kids who were more like me. I was excited about the program but really had no one to tell. Times like these were when I missed Ernestine the most.

A couple of days later, I was at lunch and one of the football players was yelling at a black girl for cutting in front of him in line. She was standing there with her head down, holding her lunch tray while he called her a stupid *n* word. I'm still not sure what possessed me, but I walked over to him and shoved him in the chest with both hands. He stumbled back, lost his balance, and sat down on the floor—hard. Everyone started laughing, and he jumped up and told me he was going to beat the hell out of me. I told him that would make him look like a big man, beating up on a little girl. He stared at me with his fists by his side, but I stood my ground. His football buddies came over and told him to leave it alone. I wasn't worth it.

I later found out that Kelli, who I played softball with, threw the kid up against a locker and told him he better not mess with me or she would get her brother, Bart, to "have a talk with him." Bart was known around town as a troublemaker. He quit school when he was sixteen, lied about his age, and started working in the oil field. I had seen him around town. He was short and stocky and had a permanent scowl. Nobody messed with him. The rumor was he had served some time in prison for cutting a man in a bar. He did, however, love his little sister, and because of him, no one messed with her. The football player never bothered me again.

After the incident in the cafeteria, I got my own reputation for being fearless. More of the kids talked to me, and I started hanging out with a group that was pretty rough. They were eleven and twelve, and I was only ten, but they didn't seem to care. They smoked and snuck liquor from their parent's liquor cabinets. I never did any of that. I stayed on the fringes of the group, mainly to have someone to sit with at lunch.

At the beginning of April, I came home from school, Mama and Daddy were both sitting at the table, and Mama had been crying. I immediately knew something was wrong.

"What? What is it?"

Daddy said, "Oh, honey."

"What? Tell me for God's sake."

"Dr. King was assassinated last night in Memphis," Daddy said.

I sat down at the table and felt this anger boil up inside of me. Ernestine had told me so many stories about Dr. King, what a good man he was, and how hard he was working to bring black and white people together to live peacefully. We had listened to his "I Have a Dream" speech together, and I remember it gave me goose bumps. What was wrong with people? I could not understand how you could kill another person for trying to make the world a better place? Where did all the hate come from?

I went into the living room and turned on the television. Walter Cronkite was talking about a man named James Earl Ray and how he had killed Dr. King. Ray had been in trouble with the law most of his life. Dr. King had been standing on the balcony of his hotel, and Ray had fired a shot out of the window of his rooming house. Dr. King died at the hospital. I turned off the TV, went to my room, and sat looking out the window. I looked at the charm of Dr. King Ernestine had given me. Everything felt completely and utterly hopeless. Things were never going to change. All the kids at my school used the *n* word and talked about the good old days when black people were slaves. I hated it, but I never said a word, which I guess made me just as bad as them. I didn't cry. There were no tears left. I was just glad Ernestine wasn't alive to witness it. Two months later, Robert Kennedy was assassinated, and I officially gave up hope that the world would someday be a better place.

A couple of weeks after Dr. King was killed, we were out of school for spring break. Most of the kids went to South Padre Island or San Antonio, but Mama and Daddy had to work, so I just stayed home, watched television, and ate junk food. My face had started breaking out, and Mama was always after me to drink more water and eat more fruits and vegetables. I liked Cheetos and Hershey bars better.

On Wednesday of spring break week, Daddy came home and said his cousin Roy; Roy's wife, Margaret; and their daughter, Donna, my second cousin, were coming for the weekend. I was excited. I had been depressed the last few weeks and was happy to have a diversion. Donna was a tomboy like me, and we always had a blast. Daddy had given me a two-seater go-cart for Christmas, which totally put Mama into outer limits. Nobody wanted to ride with me because I went too fast. Mama was constantly after me to slow down before I got myself killed, but I liked going fast.

The cousins arrived about four o'clock on Friday afternoon, and we were prepared. Mama and Daddy had left work early, and Mama went shopping to buy all the stuff for a barbecue. My Daddy made the best barbecue I had ever tasted. Everyone who ate it said he should open a restaurant. Daddy and cousin Roy started drinking about five o'clock that afternoon, and even Mama got into the swing of things and had a couple of beers. She put salt around the rim of her can and made a face every time she took a sip, but she drank them. After supper, I asked Daddy if I could take Donna around the block on my go-cart. He was crocked, so he said, "Sure! Just watch out for cars." Donna and I backed the go-cart out of the shed. I pumped the starter three times like Daddy taught me and pulled the cord. We were off. We made a couple of loops and cousin Roy flagged us down. I pulled up, and he said, "Nick, have you got a rope and a cardboard box?" Daddy said, "Probably do, out in the shed."

"Go get it," Roy said.

I could tell from looking at Roy that he was lit. Donna asked him what he was going to do. He said he was going to tie the rope to the go-cart, use the cardboard boxes like skis, and let me pull him around the block. Mama and cousin Margaret came out of the house about that time, and Margaret started telling Roy what a damn fool he was and that he was going to get himself killed. He said, "Be quiet, woman."

Daddy came around the house, waving rope and a cardboard box. They cut the sides of the box and made two flat "skis." I didn't tell Daddy or Roy that I had taken the governor off the engine, so on a straight shot, it would hit forty-five miles an hour. Roy tied the rope to the roll bar on the go-cart, held on to the other end, put the pieces of cardboard under his feet, and told me to go. I pushed the gas all the way down, and we took off. The road in our subdivision was curvy, and I could hear him yelling something, but I couldn't hear what it was. I looked back, and he was holding the rope in one hand and a beer in the other. I came around the curve in front of our house, and he lost his grip and went tumbling asshole over elbows (as my Daddy says) onto our front yard. We all rushed over to see if he was okay, and he looked at the bottom of his boots and said, "Well, I'll be damn. That road ate up the soles on my boots." We all started laughing. The adults went back to drinking and playing cards, and me and Donna went inside and watched *The Thing*. She liked scary movies too.

Later that night when I was supposed to be in bed, I was standing outside the living room door eavesdropping. Mama was saying she missed her family and friends in Louisiana. She said maybe if we moved to Jena and not Olla, it would give her some space, but she would still be close to her family. She said Roy and Margaret coming to visit made her realize that I needed to be around family. She said she was worried about the kids I was hanging out with. Daddy said moving back was fine with him. So it was decided we were moving back to Louisiana.

I finished sixth grade in Houston, but it was a blur. Our house was sold right away, so we had to stay in a hotel for two weeks until school was out. The hotel didn't allow dogs, but we snuck Lincoln in anyway. I was so happy we were going back "home" as we all called Louisiana. I knew I would have to start another new school, but all my cousins went to the school I would be attending, so at least I would know someone. We packed up and took off the day after school let out Louisiana bound!

Chapter Sixteen

We were home, and until the new wore off for Mama, it was good. I liked my school. I was in the seventh grade, and that meant junior high. There were football games and pep rallies. I was way ahead in all my classes except math. I just could not understand algebra. Why did they have to put letters in the equations? It made no sense to me. I still managed to get a B in the class and with As in everything else. My GPA wasn't too bad. Louisiana didn't have the program for gifted writers that Texas had, but other than that, school was okay.

Mama started getting antsy around Thanksgiving. We were having dinner at our house, and the whole family was coming over. Mama had people come in and clean the house from top to bottom. It was going to be a potluck, so all Mama had to make was the turkey and the rolls. When I would come home from school, she would have cookbooks spread out everywhere. I didn't know she owned a cookbook. She was a horrible cook. Her grandmother taught her how to make chicken and dumplings, and chocolate pie when she was a little girl, and she never learned anything else.

I walked in from school one afternoon, and she was wrestling with a big turkey, trying to fit it into a roasting pan that was too small.

"Christie, come hold the legs down for me."

I walked into the kitchen. I could tell from looking at the turkey that it was way too big to go in the pan she had.

"Mother, the turkey is too big for that pan. Why are you cooking a turkey now? Thanksgiving is a week away."

"I know that. I'm practicing. If you will just hold the wings and legs in, I can make if fit."

I went over and pushed the legs and wings in, and it still wouldn't fit.

"Move and let me see. Where's the twine?" Mama asked.

"Mother, I don't think twine is going to hold the legs and wings in; it will break. How many pounds is that turkey anyway?"

"Twenty-four pounds. It's the biggest one they had at the Piggly Wiggly."

"Twenty-four pounds! Good lord, Mother. What are you going to do with it for a week after it's cooked?"

"If it tastes good, I'm going to freeze it and thaw it out on Thanksgiving morning. If it tastes bad, I'll buy another one and start over."

"I don't think that will work."

"Oh, stop being such a Negative Nellie and hand me the damn twine."

Mama took the twine and wrapped it around the legs and wings several times. When she was finished, that turkey looked like it was wearing lady's corset. She stuck the meat thermometer in its side and slid it in the oven.

"Well, let's see what happens. It stays in for four hours."

I went to my room to play records and read. I must have dozed off because Mama woke me up, yelling for me to come and taste the turkey. I groaned, got up, and walked into the kitchen. The turkey was beautiful. It was golden brown, and Mama stood beside it with a butcher knife.

"Okay, I want you to taste it and give me your honest opinion."

I took the bite she handed me, and it was delicious.

"Wow. That's really good," I said.

"Really?" Mama sounded thrilled.

"Yep. You did good."

Mama began to wrap up the turkey in tin foil to freeze it for Thanksgiving Day. She was humming "My Girl" by the Temptations. She loved David Ruffin.

Thanksgiving Day was upon us, and Mama took the turkey out of the freezer that morning and put it in the oven to warm. Everyone arrived, and Mama had the table set beautifully. She brought the turkey into the dining room and everyone told her how good it looked and how much they were looking forward to trying it. Mama sat the turkey down in front of Daddy and handed him the carving knife. My cousin Dan, who we all knew would grow up to be a preacher, said the blessing, and Daddy began to carve the turkey. When he tried to put the knife in the blade bent, he looked at Mama and tried to stick the knife in a different place. This time the blade broke clean off the knife. The turkey was frozen solid. My uncle Danny said, "It's a turkey Popsicle." My mother gasped in horror and ran out of the room.

We all looked at each other, unsure what to do. Daddy stood up and told us to go ahead and start eating the rest of the food. He was just going to pop the turkey back in the oven to heat a little more. We could all hear Mama crying hysterically from the kitchen. We could hear Daddy murmuring softly. Then we heard a door slam and a car start up and back out with tires squealing. Daddy came back into the dining room.

"Betty had some errands to run so she won't be joining us for dinner."

No one said a word. Everyone in the family knew my mother leaned a little to the left. After a few seconds of silence, Daddy asked Aunt Dottie to pass the mashed potatoes, and everyone started eating and talking again. Mama didn't come home that night. I woke up around two thirty in the morning and walked into the living room. Daddy was fully clothed, lying on the sofa, sound asleep. I took a blanket out of the linen closet and covered him up. I had a sinking feeling that it was just going to be the two of us from now on.

Chapter Seventeen

The Friday after Thanksgiving, I went to my best friend Missy's house for the weekend. Missy was a year behind me in school, but we were the same age. She had three brothers, and they were always picking on us, but I loved going to her house. Her Mama was always either cooking or washing clothes. They had three big dogs that lived in the house, and usually if you spent the night over there, one of them would end up in the bed with you. Her dad was a tow truck driver, and Mama thought they were too common for me to be spending so much time with, but I didn't care. There was consistency in the chaos. Missy's mama didn't leave.

When I came home Sunday night, all of Mama's clothes were gone. I walked into hers and Daddy's bedroom and stood looking in the half-empty closet. She hadn't even said goodbye this time. I had no idea where Daddy was. I went to the kitchen and started pulling out Thanksgiving leftovers. I ate by myself in front of the television. I must have fallen asleep because Daddy woke me up when he came home, rip-roaring drunk. I tried to get him to eat, but he refused. He sat down on the couch and stared at me.

"Well, she's gone again," He said.

"Where?"

"Hell, if I know. Said the domesticated life wasn't for her. Said she was a lousy cook, lousy wife, and lousy mother. Said she should have never got married and had a kid. Well, you know what I say? To hell with her! We can make it just fine by ourselves. Did it before, and we can do it again by God. It's just you and me, kiddo."

Then he promptly fell over, passed out, and started snoring.

I knew deep down inside that Mama never really wanted me. She liked to dress me up and show me off, but she didn't mother me like other kid's mothers did. She almost treated me like a toy that she could take out and play with when she felt like it. It still hurt to know for sure she didn't want me. I was eleven years old and basically on my own. I knew Daddy wasn't going to be any help. He was falling apart, and she had only been gone a few days. I could go live with my grandparents, but I would have to leave my friends and change schools again. Plus they were strict and went to church a lot. I decided to just stick it out with Daddy and hope for the best. In six more years, I would be headed to college at LSU, and after that I would be a famous writer living in New York. I figured I could hang in there that long.

I began to spend more and more time at Missy's house. Her parents knew my situation, so they kind of unofficially adopted me. I ate many meals at their house and spent countless nights on their hide-a-bed. They always made me feel wanted. They were the family I wished I'd had. I went home every third day or so to clean up and wash Daddy's clothes. He spent most nights at The Lamplighter bar. By some miracle, he managed to stay sober during the day, so he wouldn't get fired, but after work was another story.

About two weeks after Mama left, I received a postcard from San Antonio. She said she was a hostess at a family restaurant, and she would send for me as soon as she was settled. I threw it away without mentioning it to Daddy. He never said if he knew where she was or not, but I wasn't going to be the one to tell him.

One Friday afternoon when Mama had been gone about six months, I came home from school; and when I walked in the back door, I could hear Daddy talking to someone. It was a woman. I put my books on the table and walked into the living room. I could only see the back of her head, but her hair was jet-black and cut in a bob. Daddy saw me and stood up.

"Christie, this is Diane."

The woman stood up, turned to me, and stuck out her hand for me to shake. I shook her hand. It was very soft.

"I'm so happy to meet you. Your Dad talks about you nonstop."

"Does he?"

"He sure does. He told me that you are extremely smart and a very good softball player."

I was in awe of this woman. She smelled like magnolias, and she was very soft-spoken and very pretty. She was wearing a suit like businessmen wore. I was intensely curious.

Daddy coughed and said, "Diane is the marketing director for our company. She works in the head office in Houston, but she's been here for a couple of months working with us to create a new ad campaign. She was tired of eating out, so I invited her over for one of my famous barbecue steaks. Why don't you two get acquainted and I'll go fire up the ole grille. Christie, I bought some wine. Could you pour Diane a glass?"

Wine? My Dad had never bought wine in his life, not that I knew of anyway. I walked into the kitchen and took the wine out of the fridge. It had a cork in it. I had no idea how to get the cork out. I grabbed a steak knife and started trying to dig it out. I ended up pushing the cork into the bottle. I grabbed a mason jar and poured wine to the top. There were little pieces of cork in it, but I hoped Diane wouldn't notice. I took an Orange Crush out of the fridge and walked back into the living room.

"Here you go," I said. I handed her the glass.

"Um, thank you."

I sat down across from her, and we both took sips from our drinks.

"So did you go to college?" I asked.

"Yes, I graduated from the University of Texas. I'm a Longhorn."

"What was your major?"

"Marketing and business."

"I'm going to go to LSU to major in creative writing. I want to be a writer like Harper Lee."

"Wow, that's great! I love Harper Lee."

While Daddy was cooking, I told her about starting school when I was four and how I hated always being the youngest in the class. I told her about my friends and all about Ernestine and how much

I missed her. I talked to her about everything except my mother. I didn't mention her at all.

Daddy stuck his head in the door and said the steaks and potatoes were almost done. Daddy made these sliced potatoes and onions on the grille that were amazing. He asked me to make a salad. I didn't want to stop talking to Diane. I hadn't talked to anyone that much since Ernestine died. Diane told me she wasn't much of a cook, but she thought she could probably help throw a salad together. We went into the kitchen. I washed the lettuce and tore it into pieces, and she cut up the tomatoes.

By the time Daddy brought the food in, we had the table set and the salad ready. We all sat down to eat, and there were no awkward silences like there used to be when Mama was at the table. We all talked and laughed, and the night went way too fast. Diane and I cleaned up the kitchen, then she and Daddy had coffee, and we all talked some more. Finally, around ten o'clock, Diane got up to leave.

"Christie, I have thoroughly enjoyed spending time with you. I was planning to drive over to Alexandria tomorrow to do some shopping at the mall. It looks like I'm going to be in town a while longer, and I need something to wear besides suits. Would you like to go with me?"

My heart started beating fast. She liked me. She wanted to spend more time with me!

"That would be great. Thanks."

"Good. I will pick you up around ten in the morning."

"Okay. Good night."

"Good night."

Daddy walked her out to her car, and I ran to my room to figure out what I was going to wear for our shopping trip.

Chapter Eighteen

Diane showed up at ten on the dot the next morning. She came in and had a cup of coffee with Daddy while I finished getting ready. She was wearing a pair of gray wool trousers, a white button down shirt, and black ballet flats. I was wearing my best pair of Levi's, a button-down shirt like hers except it was light blue, and my black ballet flats. When I saw how similar we were dressed, I was excited that we had the same taste in clothes. I walked into the kitchen.

"Well, look how adorable you are."

"Thank you."

"I was thinking about getting a trim today as well. My hair is too long and is starting to fall in my eyes. Would you like me to make an appointment for you too? We could go after lunch and the mall."

I hadn't had my hair cut in over a year. Mama had given up on turning me into a girl, so I basically just brushed it all back and pulled it into a ponytail. I really wanted a cut like Sharon Tate in *Valley of the Dolls* but was unsure how it would look. I thought the kids at school might make fun of me. I was more popular than I had ever been, mainly because Missy was my best friend and she was friends with everyone, but I was still nervous about making any radical changes in my appearance. I thought about it for a minute and decided to go for it.

"That would be great!"

"I will go make the appointments now."

Diane went into the other room to use the phone.

Daddy said, "Well, you two seem to be getting along really well."

"Yeah, she's really cool. She's nothing like Mama."

"No, no, she's not."

Daddy looked sad, and I felt bad for saying that, but it was true. Diane was confident and had her act together. She had a great sense of humor, and I bet she never would have left her husband and daughter just because the turkey was frozen. Diane would have laughed it off and said, "Well, everyone fill up on mashed potatoes." I wanted to be like her.

She came back into the kitchen.

"We're all set. Are you ready to go?"

"Yes, ma'am."

"Oh please, just call me Diane. You make me feel old when you call me ma'am."

She put her arm around my shoulders, and we walked out to her car.

It was the best day of my life. We went to the mall, and I bought a couple of dresses. Yes, after all the time Mama spent trying to get me into dresses, I picked a couple I liked. Diane was a big help. She knew what colors and styles looked good on me. She bought more trousers and a dress. Then we went to lunch at A&W. I loved their root beer floats, and Diane did too. She wasn't worried about her figure, which was a welcome relief from Mama. We talked about everything—books and how I wanted to be a famous writer. She told me about Virginia Woolf and Sylvia Plath and how they were both tortured and how they killed themselves. I couldn't wait to go to the library and check out their books.

We went to the hairdresser, and Diane got a trim. Her hair was cut like Barbara Streisand's. It was short and framed her face. I told the lady what I wanted, and when she was finished, I was shocked. For the first time in my life, I felt pretty. My hair hung in waves around my shoulders, and I had bangs, which kept me from looking too old. I absolutely loved it.

"You look beautiful," said Diane, and I believed her.

We made it home around four o'clock. Daddy was shocked when he saw me but recovered nicely. He said I looked so grown up. He invited Diane to dinner, but she said she had some work to do, so we invited her to come over the next day for spaghetti Sunday and she agreed. When I went to school Monday, everyone told me I looked great and several of the boys said hi to me. It was the first time I understood the power women have over men.

The next Saturday, Diane and I planned to go see a movie. We were going to see *Rosemary's Baby*. Diane liked scary movies too. My birthday had come and gone. Daddy gave me twenty dollars. Mama sent me a pink purse that I pushed to the back of my closet. Diane found out somehow and gave me a thin gold chain with a book charm on it. It was my most prized possession other than Ernestine's charm bracelet that I still wore every day. Christmas was coming up, and Diane was going back to Houston to spend the holidays with her family. I wasn't sure what hers and Daddy's relationship was, but they laughed a lot.

The movie was great, and we both agreed Mia Farrow was a great actress. The director of the film, Roman Polanski, was married to Sharon Tate, who I loved. They were going to have a baby. I followed their lives in the tabloid magazines. Diane left to go back to Houston, and it was just me and Daddy again. We were both a little lost without Diane's bright personality and silly jokes, but we didn't talk about it. Christmas came and went.

Mama called Christmas morning, but I refused to talk to her. Daddy didn't have much to say to her either. I did hear him tell her maybe it was time they both moved on with their lives, but I'm not sure what she said, and I didn't ask. I didn't know anyone whose parents were divorced, but I found I felt ambivalent about it. Mama had never really been a part of my life. She parented at arm's length, so it was hard to miss what I never really had. Diane called on New Year's Eve, and we both felt happier after talking to her. She was coming back to town the next week. Daddy and I rang in 1969, playing cards and listening to the countdown in New York. It was easy and comfortable, and we were both content.

Chapter Nineteen

Diane came back into town, and things resumed as before. She came over to the house a couple of times a week for dinner. Usually, she and I went to a movie or shopping on the weekends. I got my ears pierced. We all knew her time with us was almost up. She had finished the ad campaign, and it was doing well on television and the radio. The last week of May, she told Daddy and me at dinner that she would be heading back to Houston the next week. I tried to send Daddy telepathic messages to ask her to stay, but he didn't pick up on them.

"We will miss you, but I hope you'll come visit us," Daddy said.

Diane gave Daddy a funny look and softly said, "Of course, I will."

Later, she and I were doing the dishes, and I decided to ask her what the relationship was between her and Daddy.

"So what's the deal with you and Daddy?"

She didn't say anything for a long time, just kept drying the plates.

"I care for your father very much, Christie, but I'll never win. I can't compete with your mother."

"What? She's not even here. She left us. She didn't want us. Daddy doesn't love her anymore."

"Oh, I think he does. Some people only love one person their entire lives, and that's how it is with your parents. They can't be together, but they can't let go of each other either. I will miss you terribly, but it's time for me to go home."

I hugged her and cried. "I don't want you to."

She hugged me back. “I know, sweet girl. I know. Would you like to come to Houston for a couple of weeks this summer and visit me?”

I said yes into her shoulder. She pulled me away and grabbed my face, looking into my eyes.

“Christie, you are extraordinary. You are smart and beautiful and kind, and you want so desperately for the world to be a good place. Don’t ever let anyone extinguish your light. I believe I will be reading your novels one day, and I hope you will invite me to New York to visit.”

“I will,” I said.

She hugged me tightly again, grabbed her purse, said goodbye to Daddy, and walked out. Daddy and I looked at each other.

I totally lost it.

“You’re an idiot for letting her go! Mama is never coming back, and even if she does, I don’t want her here. It’s over! She doesn’t love us and never did. Can’t you see that?”

“Christie Ann, I know you’re upset, but don’t talk to me that way. Marriage is complicated. You will understand when you’re older.”

“I know Mom aren’t supposed to leave! I know that much, and she’s done it twice. Who the hell does she think she is to come in and out of our lives that way? Does she have any idea how much it hurts to know your own mother wishes you were never born?” I ran from the room crying, went into my bedroom, and slammed the door.

A little while later, Daddy knocked on my door, but I told him to go away. I hated my mother and that fury filled me until nothing else was left. She still had control over us even though she was hundreds of miles away. I wished Daddy would divorce her and marry Diane so I could have a real mother. A mother that wanted me and wouldn’t leave.

I finished seventh grade and convinced our veterinarian, Dr. Roose, to let me work for him cleaning out kennels and bathing dogs. It was cool because Lincoln could come with me. I loved being around all the animals, and for a while, I thought about becoming a veterinarian instead of a writer; but when I realized I would have to put animals to sleep, I decided to stick with writing.

I spent a lot of time with friends that summer, swimming, watching movies, and hanging out at Mitchell's restaurant. I was excited to start eighth grade because the accelerated program they had in Texas for students who were good in English and writing had finally made it to Jena. The program was for eighth grade through twelfth grade. I planned to be in the program all five years. I had also learned I would be a contributing reporter for the Campus Cruiser, our school's newspaper. It was a fun summer, but I was ready to move onto the last year of junior high.

I took the money I made at the vet's office and the hundred dollars Daddy gave me and bought new school clothes. I missed having Diane help me shop. She had the ability to choose things I never would have picked out but looked good on me. We spoke on the phone once a week, and she sent me funny cards and little gifts, but they couldn't take the place of having her with me in person. Daddy stopped going to bars and became really focused on his job. He went on a couple of dates. He and Mother had decided they could date other people. It was a strange marriage, but I didn't care enough to question it. I had begun to say Mother or Betty when I had to say her name at all, which was very little. Daddy got onto me at first but finally realized it was a losing battle. I threw her letters away unopened and refused to speak to her on the phone. If she didn't want me, then I didn't want her either. It hardly even hurt anymore.

Chapter Twenty

In eighth grade, I had my first boyfriend. His name was Hollis Black, and he was in my social studies class. He started talking to me the first day of school and never stopped. He looked a little like Paul McCartney but without the hair and the English accent. The Beatles were one of my favorite bands, so the attraction was mutual. We started eating lunch together and meeting each other at the football games. We held hands and were voted "cutest couple of the month" in October of that year. I really didn't feel one way or the other about having a boyfriend. All my friends had one, and Hollis was nice. He never pressured me into doing anything I didn't want to do. I spent half of our time together worried he was going to try to kiss me. I heard girls in the locker room, after softball practice, talking about going to second base, but I had no idea what that meant. I decided to ask my aunt Dottie.

We went to Aunt Dottie and Uncle Danny's house a lot. Daddy and Aunt Dottie were brother and sister. The next time we were at their house, I caught Aunt Dottie alone in the kitchen.

"Aunt Dottie, can I ask you something?"

"Sure. Ask away."

"What does it mean when a guy says he got to second base?"

"Why? Have you been on second base?"

"No! I just heard it at school, and I wanted to know what it means."

"Well, it's just a way to explain certain types of intimate contact."

I wasn't sure what that meant.

"You mean like kissing?"

"Well, technically, first base is a kiss, second base is someone touching your breast under your bra, third base is someone touching your monkey [Aunt Dottie's word for *vagina*. Mother insisted on calling body parts by their actual name], and fourth base is having sex."

I thought about it for a moment. Now baseball was ruined for me.

"So have you been on any of those bases?"

"No! All Hollis does is hold my hand. I don't want to run the bases."

Then Aunt Dottie sat me down and explained the birds and bees to me. Mama had already told me most of it, but Aunt Dottie added some things I promised myself I would never do. I was sorry I brought it up. I knew older sisters of my friends who got pregnant in high school and ended up living in a trailer with a baby and a husband who was always out with his friends. They never left Jena. They just stayed there and had more babies and married different husbands. I saw them in the grocery store sometimes, and they always looked sad.

The homecoming football game and dance were a big deal in junior high. Eighth graders could attend the dance at the high school, so two weeks before the event, my aunt Elaine took me to Alexandria to buy a dress. She was my daddy's other sister. She filled in when I needed something girly. We spent all day going to different shops, but I couldn't find what I wanted. I had an idea in my head of what I wanted to look like, and none of the dresses I tried on fit that idea. Finally, at the last store we went to, I found it. It was a champagne color with a full skirt and capped sleeves. It hugged my waist and ended right above my knees. I looked at Aunt Elaine, and she nodded at me. We both knew this was the one. Aunt Elaine paid for the dress, and we went on a search for shoes.

The big night finally arrived, and I put the dress on. Aunt Dottie and Aunt Elaine came over and curled my hair and helped with my makeup. When I walked down the hall and Daddy looked up and saw me, he had big tears in his eyes.

"Is that my little girl?"

"It's me, Daddy."

"You look beautiful, Sunshine."

"Thank you."

The doorbell rang. Daddy went and opened it, and Hollis stood there in a suit that looked a little big for him in the shoulders. When he saw me, his eyes got big. Daddy invited him in and then took a ton of pictures. Hollis's dad finally came to the door looking for us. His parents were going to take us to the dance, and Daddy was going to pick us up. I had never met Hollis's parents before. When I got in the car, his mom turned and smiled at me.

"You look lovely, Christie. It's so nice to finally meet you."

"Thank you. You too."

It was only a ten-minute drive to the school, and Hollis's dad made lame jokes the entire way. Hollis's parents were just like him—nice. We made it to the school, thanked them for the ride, and jumped out. Hollis grabbed my hand as we walked into the gymnasium. I couldn't believe it was the same place where I attended basketball camp each summer. There were lighted lanterns hanging from the ceiling and crepe paper roses everywhere. The tables had candles. A slow song was playing, so Hollis pulled me onto the dance floor, grabbed my arms, and put them around his neck. He put his hands on my waist, and we started moving in that slow-motion circle that kids at their first dance do. For some reason, I thought of my mother and wished she was there to see me looking "girly." I still liked to do boy things, but being a girl wasn't so bad either.

All our friends began to arrive, and everyone looked so nice. The boys kept pulling at their shirt collars, not accustomed to wearing ties and jackets. Hollis and I sat at one of the tables in the front, sometimes dancing and sometimes content just to watch everyone else. It was a magical night, and before I knew it, it was over. We walked out to the parking lot where Daddy was waiting. I was beginning to think going to first base might not be so bad.

Hollis and I continued as a couple through eighth grade. He came over on Saturday afternoons, and we would sit outside in the swing at the back of the house away from my father's prying eyes. He finally kissed me on Valentine's Day, and it was sweet and innocent just as your first kiss should be. We kissed a few times after that, but we were both happy to just sit, hold hands, and talk about what we wanted for the future. Hollis wanted to join the air force and be a fighter pilot. He believed that the war in Vietnam would be over soon and said he would probably end up dropping food supplies to soldiers overseas. He didn't think he would ever be in combat. He knew I wanted to go to LSU, be a famous writer, and live in New York City. We were both smart enough to know we were too young to make long-term promises. We enjoyed the now of our relationship and that was enough.

Eighth grade ended, and Diane invited me to come and stay with her for two weeks in Houston. Hollis and I made promises to see each other over the summer, but I think we both knew our childhood love affair had run its course. It was bittersweet. On the last day of school, we signed each other's yearbooks. He wrote, "To my first love. I'm so glad it was you." In his, I wrote, "Thanks for the memories. Good luck in high school." Romantic, I know. I still had problems with that kind of stuff.

Chapter Twenty-One

I left for Houston two days after school was out. It was my first time to fly on an airplane. It was cool, and I felt very grown up, navigating the airport on my own. Diane was waiting at the gate when I walked off the plane, and she ran and gave me a big hug. I only had one carry-on bag because she said I could wash clothes at her house, and she planned to take me on a shopping trip anyway. We went outside to her car, and it looked just like I thought it would. It was a red convertible Mustang. I climbed in, Diane turned the radio up, and we headed to her apartment. When we arrived, she left the car with a doorman who was in front of her building. She introduced me. His name was Clive, and he said he had heard all about me and was happy I was visiting Ms. Diane. We took the elevator to the seventh floor, which opened onto a marble hallway. I tried not to let my mouth hang open, but so far everything was amazing.

We stopped in front of number 7002. Diane opened the door and let me walk in first. It was different from anything I had ever seen. Everything was white with splashes of red. She had a red vase sitting on the glass coffee table and red pillows on the sofa. The rug in the hallway was red and fluffy. It was beautiful. She walked me down the hall to the guest room where I would be staying. There was a four-poster bed with a blue and yellow quilt. There were yellow curtains on the windows and a white wicker chair with yellow and blue pillows. There was a little nightstand by the bed that matched the wicker chair. It had a yellow lamp and a water pitcher with a glass sitting on it. The bathroom was right off the bedroom, and there were fluffy yellow towels and all kinds of lotions and soaps. I was entranced. I loved all of it. There wasn't one thing I would change.

"Do you like it?"

"I love it!" I said.

"Good. I wanted it to be pretty but not girly. I know you don't like that."

"Actually, I've started doing a few girly things. I went to the homecoming dance—with a boy!"

"What? Oh my gosh, I can't wait to hear all about it. Why don't you unpack and meet me in the kitchen? I picked up some boiled shrimp and potatoes for us. I remember when we went to lunch one time, you picked the boiled shrimp. I hope these taste as good."

I walked over and hugged Diane tightly and told her thank-you. She hugged me back and told me she was glad I was there.

Diane had to work the next morning, but she was taking half a day off to take me to a Houston Astros game. John Mayberry was my favorite player because we both played first base. He had been playing in the minors and the majors, but he was on the roster today, and I was superexcited to see him. He was born in Detroit, and Daddy told me Detroit was called the Motor City because that's where all the cars were made. Our Chevrolet Nova was made there.

The game was supposed to start at one o'clock. Diane came home at noon with a Houston Astros T-shirt for me to wear. When I was little, the New York Yankees were my team, but that was mainly because they were Daddy's team. When we lived in Houston, the Astros were always on television, and I started watching them. They were my team now. Daddy still loved the Yankees, but he said the Astros were his second favorite. We drove downtown, parked in a lot where a man was charging five dollars to "watch our car," and then walked to the park. It was a beautiful day, not too hot, and there was a light breeze blowing. There were people walking beside us and behind us, and they were all wearing Houston Astros T-shirts and baseball caps. Everyone seemed to be in a good mood, and it was easy to get caught up in the excitement.

We gave our tickets to the man at the gate and walked down the corridor toward our seats. Diane suggested we get our hot dogs now so we wouldn't miss any of the game later. After purchasing our food, we walked through the gate, and the field unfolded before me. It was huge! The grass was so green. Some of the players were on the field, warming up, and people were yelling at them for autographs. Some of the players went over and signed some baseballs and bats. We found our seats and waited for the game to start. It was a squeaker, but Houston pulled it out in the ninth inning with a walk off home run. Everyone was going crazy.

Since that day, I have been to hundreds of baseball games. I even saw the Atlanta Braves win the World Series, but no game has ever topped that one. The taste of the hot dog, the ice-cold Coke, everyone yelling at the umpires about what they perceived to be a bad call, the crack of the bat—it was a magical day and cemented my love for baseball.

Diane and I walked back to her car and headed home. We talked nonstop the entire way. Diane was a big baseball fan too, but her favorite team was the Boston Red Sox because she grew up in Boston. I told her I wouldn't hold the fact that she was a Yankee against her. When we got back to her condo, she said she had about an hour's worth of work to do, so I grabbed a towel and went downstairs to hang out by the pool. I thought how great it would be if Diane was my mom. I felt a little disloyal to my mother but not much. She had finally stopped writing and calling me. I overheard Daddy tell Aunt Dottie that Mama was working in an office and she was the manager. I could have cared less. I never asked Daddy about her, and he knew better than to mention her in front of me.

The rest of my visit was a blur, laying out by the pool, clothes shopping, eating at nice restaurants, and meeting all of Diane's friends. Before I knew it, my last day arrived. Diane had mentioned a boyfriend, but I had never met him. Diane decided to give me a going-away party, so she invited her friends I had gotten to know, a couple of kids from the condo complex I had been hanging around with at the pool, and her boyfriend. I was curious about him. All Diane said about him was "he's in management."

Diane went all out and decorated the condo with streamers and balloons. She had nonalcoholic strawberry daiquiris for us kids, and the adults drank beer and margaritas. She ordered food from the Mexican restaurant I had come to love. Everything was perfect. About an hour into the party, the doorbell rang; and when Diane opened the door, I saw a big man wearing a black Western shirt with Wrangler jeans and cowboy boots. She brought him over to me.

"Jake, this is Christie."

He held out his hand, and I shook it. He maintained eye contact a couple of seconds too long.

"Well, Diane was right. You are a beautiful young lady."

Diane excused herself to get him a beer, and he stood there continuing to stare at me. This guy was giving me the serious creeps.

"So have you had a good time? I bet Houston's a lot different than what you're used to."

"Not really. Just bigger. I think people are pretty much the same everywhere."

He threw his head back and laughed loudly. I wasn't sure what the joke was, so I just smiled.

"Diane told me you were a precocious little thing. Said you just say what you think and don't care who likes it or not."

I didn't know what to say, so I just stood there. Where was Diane? Finally, she appeared and handed him a beer. She told me my friends had opened the sparklers and were out on the balcony. I excused myself and went to join them. For the rest of the night, every time I looked up, Jake was staring at me. When the party was starting to wind down, I went into my bedroom to get a sweatshirt. The night had turned cold. When I turned around, Jake was standing there.

"Get cold, did ya?"

He was slurring his words, and I could tell he was really drunk. He reached over and grabbed a strand of my hair.

"You sure are pretty. You ever been kissed?"

I didn't say anything. I wanted to leave, but he was blocking the door. I told him I needed to get back to the party, but he just kept standing there. He grabbed my hand and pulled me toward him. I stumbled into him. Before I knew what was happening, he grabbed the back of my head, bent down, and stuck his tongue in my mouth. I froze. Hollis and I had kissed but never French-kissed. I put my hands on his chest and pushed him away. He tried to grab me again, but I scooted across my bed and slid down the wall in the corner. He stood their swaying, staring at me. "You better not tell Diane about this. I'd hate to have to tell her what a little tease you are." He turned around and walked out. I sat down on the floor and started shaking. A few minutes later, Diane came in looking for me.

"Honey, are you okay? You're as white as a sheet."

I so wanted to tell her, but I was afraid she would believe him over me. I told her I had come in to get a sweatshirt because I caught a chill on the balcony.

"Well, people are starting to leave, so you better come out and tell everyone goodbye."

She stared at me for another minute and walked out. I stood up and walked into the living room. I hugged everyone and thanked them for coming. When Jake was ready to leave, he said, "Don't I get a hug?" I walked up to him and gave him a side hug. He whispered in my ear that I better keep my mouth shut; then he was gone.

I told Diane I was tired and wanted to get to bed early so I would be awake to catch my flight the next morning. She hugged me and kissed me on the top of the head. I almost told her then, but I didn't. The wonderful two weeks I had spent with Diane were ruined. All I would ever remember about the trip was the awful taste of Jake's beer breath and his big, sloppy tongue stuck down my throat. At that moment, I missed my mother. I needed to talk to someone and find out what I should do. I worried about Diane. If Jake had done that to me, he was probably doing it to other people. Diane deserved so much better. I felt big teardrops sliding down my face. I must have cried myself to sleep because the next thing I knew, Diane was telling me to wake up. I had packed the day before, so I was ready to go. Diane had bought me so many new clothes. I had to borrow one of her suitcases to carry everything home. On the way to the airport, she kept asking me if everything was okay. I told her I was fine that I was just tired. She told me she couldn't wait for me to come back next summer, but I knew that my time with Diane was over. The secret between us was just too big. She walked me to my gate and hugged me goodbye. I boarded the plane for home.

Chapter Twenty-Two

I started my freshman year at Jena High School in 1970. My mother sent me a Beatles T-shirt and a card. I put the T-shirt at the back of my dresser drawer and threw the card away. Diane called a couple of times, but when I couldn't carry on my end of the conversation, she gave up. She sent me a long letter telling me how wonderful I was and that I could tell her anything and she would understand. I read and reread it, crying each time. I finally put it at the back of my drawer with the Beatles T-shirt.

High school wasn't as exciting as I thought it would be. As a freshman, I was at the bottom of the ladder and was pretty much ignored by the upperclassman. I worked on the school newspaper, and my article about the daily life of a freshman garnered me my own column. I signed up for the yearbook staff and begin working out so I would be ready for softball tryouts when the time came. Hollis and I saw each other in the hall and said hello, but that was it. He was dating a sophomore, and they were always standing at her locker, kissing.

One Saturday morning, I was at the school track, running laps, when someone standing at the fence yelled my name. I looked over and saw Charles Jones. I knew who he was; everyone did. He was a senior and captain of the football team. I didn't even know he knew who I was. He was dating this tough girl named Tammy Milligan, and she made it very clear what she would do to someone stupid enough to mess with her boyfriend. He motioned for me to come over to the fence. I knew I looked horrible. I wasn't wearing any makeup. My hair was in a ponytail, and I was sweating all over the place. I walked up to the fence and said hi.

"Hi. I'm Charles."

"Yeah, I know."

He laughed a little and said, "And you're Christie."

I said, "Guilty as charged."

He laughed again.

"Christie, I heard you're a really good writer, and I need a really good writer."

"What do you mean?"

"Well, I have a D in American history, and if I don't get it up to a B, I won't be able to play football. I was hoping you could help me out."

"You want me to write a paper for you?" I was incredulous. That was cheating!

"No, not write it, just kind of point me in the right direction. Actually, I think I'm going to need help most of the year. I would be happy to pay you. I can write the papers if you could just read over them when I'm finished and maybe make them a little better."

I thought about it for a minute. He wasn't asking me to write the paper. He just needed some help editing it.

"I guess I could do that."

"Great. I have one in my car. Can I give it to you? It's due Monday."

I said sure, and he ran out to his car and came back with a wadded-up piece of paper.

"How long are the papers supposed to be?" I asked.

"Three to five pages. This is an outline. I just need help filling it in."

"What's the subject?"

"The Holocaust."

I was intrigued. I had read several books about the Holocaust and knew I could write the paper solely based on what I already knew. I told him to come by my house at one o'clock and I would help him.

"That would be great! Can we just keep this between us? I don't want Tammy to think I'm doing something I shouldn't be." Then he laughed again.

"Fine with me. I'll see you at one."

I finished up my run, went home and took a shower. I didn't go out of my way to look nice. This wasn't a date. I wore my oldest pair of Levi's and an LSU T-shirt. I put on some clear lip gloss and a little mascara, but that was it. At five minutes until one, the doorbell rang. I walked over and opened the door, and there he was holding his history book and that crumpled piece of paper. I invited him in and asked if he wanted something to drink. He said a glass of tea would be good, so I went into the kitchen and poured a glass for each of us. When I went back into the living room, he was looking at a framed picture on the wall of me, Mama, and Daddy. In the picture, I was four.

"How come no one ever sees your mama?"

"I don't have a mama."

"Oh, I'm sorry. Did she pass?"

"Nope."

I sat down at the dining table and told him to give me the book and his "outline." The first thing I did was teach him how to write an outline; then I went through the chapters with him showing him how to pull the main idea out of each paragraph. Then I told him what the paper should say. He wrote it down verbatim. When we were finished, I thought it was a pretty good paper. I didn't want to make it too good because I knew Mr. Thompson would never believe he wrote it. It was a solid B+ paper. When we finished, he stood up to go?

"Thanks for your help. I have another paper due in a couple of weeks. Can you help me with that one too?"

I told him that was fine and that was how it started. He came over every other Saturday, and on the third Saturday, we begin to talk about things other than history. He told me he had never known his dad; he had run off when Charles was just a baby. He said it was just him, his mom, and his sister. His mom worked doing laundry and ironing rich people's clothes. He said he wanted to go to LSU and study engineering. I told him I wanted to be a writer. I didn't tell him about Mama. I didn't like to talk about it, and I certainly didn't want it all over school. My best friend Missy knew and that was it. On the fifth Saturday, he started talking about Tammy, how possessive she was, and how mad she would get if he even talked to another girl. He said he was going to break up with her. On the seventh Saturday, he asked if he could kiss me. I nodded my head yes. He leaned over, opened my lips with his tongue, stuck it in my mouth, and moved it around real slow. It was a French kiss, but it was nothing like Jake's. It was very soft and nice.

He pulled back and said, "Whoa. I shouldn't have done that. You're too young, and I haven't officially broken up with Tammy yet."

I told him it was okay, and this time I was the one who leaned over and kissed him.

When he left that day, he asked me to go to the movies with him the next Friday. He said he was going to go over to Tammy's and break up with her as soon as he left my house. I told him I would love to go to the movies with him. He kissed me again and left. I was officially in love. I called Missy and gave her all the details. She squealed and told me how happy she was for me.

The following Monday, Missy and I walked up to the square (the square was where everyone hung out. We called it the square because, get this, it was a big square). I looked over to where Charles usually sat and saw Tammy sitting on his lap with her arms around his neck. They were laughing about something. I felt physically ill. I grabbed Missy's arm and ran to the bathroom. I felt like a fool. He never meant to break up with Tammy. He just wanted to make out with me. Many of the older boys called me Ice Princess because I didn't make out with people and date someone new every other week. Later that day, I was at my locker and Tammy and some of her friends walked up. Tammy slammed my locker door, almost catching my finger.

"You will never get him, bitch. He's mine."

They all laughed and yelled Ice Princess and walked off. My hands were shaking. I almost called Daddy and told him I was sick and to come get me, but I didn't. I wasn't going to let some little nobody scare me. I saw Charles walking down the hall toward my locker. He kept looking behind himself to see if Tammy was around. When he got to my locker, he said, "I tried to break up with her, but she threatened to kill herself. She has emotional problems. I've got to take it slow. Can you still help me with my paper?"

I slammed my locker door and looked him straight in the eye.

"Go to hell, and give your little emotionally unstable girlfriend a message for me. If she ever comes near me again, I will slap the taste out of her mouth. Are we clear?"

His eyes were big, but he shook his head yes.

"Good. Now if you will excuse me, I need to get to English class."

I could feel his eyes on me as I walked down the hall, but I didn't care. Ernestine raised me to understand my own worth, and no one was going to treat me the way he did. I didn't care if I never had a boyfriend.

The days rolled along. My birthday and Christmas came and went. Mama sent me a makeup kit from Merle Norman, where she was working now, and a long letter. I used the makeup kit, but I threw the letter away without reading it. Daddy gave me some jeans and a coat I had asked for. The coat was cool. It was army green and looked like the one soldiers wore. I loved it. He also gave me a book about the birds and the bees, but Aunt Dottie had taken care of that a long time ago. The pictures were interesting to look at. I couldn't imagine ever doing any of it with a boy. I would be too embarrassed.

I tried out for the school softball team and made it. I played first base. I wasn't a starter because I was only a freshman, but I still played quite a bit. Charles's girlfriend, Tammy, was on the team. He had never broken up with her, and she wore his class ring on a chain around her neck. I would catch her staring at me sometimes, and I would stare back until she averted her eyes. She never said anything else to me. Our team was good, and we made it all the way to the state playoffs before we lost to a team from Gonzalez. Those girls were huge! It was still cool to be state runner-up.

The school year ended, and I went back to work at the veterinarian's office. Diane called and invited me to come stay a couple of weeks in Houston, but I told her I was working. She said, "Maybe next year."

One night, Daddy came home from work and told me he needed to talk to me. I was making dinner. I had long since taken over keeping the house clean, grocery shopping, and making dinner.

"What's up?" I asked.

"Let's sit down."

"What's wrong? Did somebody die?"

"No, no, everybody's fine. It's about your mother."

"Then I don't want to hear it."

"Christie, she's sick. She has ovarian cancer. It's pretty bad."

I just looked at him. Cancer. Even I knew that most people didn't recover from cancer.

"They've given her six months to a year. She doesn't have anybody in San Antonio to take care of her, so she is going to come live with us. I'm going to take a leave of absence from work."

"What? I don't want her here, and I sure as hell am not taking care of her. Why on earth would you want to take care of that woman? After everything she's done to you, to us?"

"I've loved her since I was nineteen, and I still love her. I'm not going to let her die alone. You don't have to take care of her or even speak to her if you don't want to, but I'm going to pick her up on Saturday, and I want you to go with me."

"Like hell I will."

I went to my bedroom and slammed the door. How was I supposed to hate someone who was dying? I had carried so much hate and rage in my heart for so long. I didn't know any other way to feel about her. Daddy could bring her here, there was nothing I could do about that, but I was not going to be nice to her.

Chapter Twenty-Three

Daddy left bright and early the next Saturday headed for San Antonio. I went over to Missy's house to lie out by their pool. I told her what was going on.

"Christie, I don't want to make you mad, but for your own sake, you need to let that hate go."

"What the hell are you talking about?"

"You're my best friend, and I love you, but you have this wall around you. There are a lot of boys at school who want to ask you out, including my brother, but they're afraid to. When you speak to people, you are sarcastic and sometimes just downright mean. Aren't you tired of being mad all the time?"

"Missy, I love you, so I'm going to let that slide. How would you feel if your mother left you not once but twice and then you found out she never really wanted you in the first place? Does your brother really want to go out with me?"

"Yes, but that would be weird, so put it out of your head. I just think it might be time to cut your mom a little bit of slack, that's all."

For the rest of the afternoon, I kept thinking about what Missy said. It was always in the back of my mind. It was like a toothache. You knew it was going to hurt, but you kept sticking your tongue in it anyway. I knew the right thing to do was forgive my mother, but I just could not soften my heart toward her. I was so angry and so hurt and had carried those feelings around for so long; it had become a badge of honor. I wanted my mother to understand that when she left, something inside of me that was innocent and trusting had been broken. Nothing could ever make that go away. I hated her for leaving me and forcing me to grow up long before I should have. I wanted to yell and scream at her and make her feel as bad as I did, but now she was dying, and I felt like I'd lost my chance to tell her what she did to me. Part of me never wanted to see her again, but another part of me wanted her to cry and beg for forgiveness just so I could refuse to give it. Daddy would be back with her the next day. I wondered what she looked like. Was she still beautiful? What would it be like when we saw each other? I fell asleep that night on Missy's couch with a knot in my stomach, wondering what tomorrow would bring.

The next day around five o'clock, I headed home. I knew Daddy was supposed to be home with her around four. When I walked in the back door, I could hear voices. It was my dad and my grandparents, and I could faintly hear my mother's voice. I walked into the living room, and my grandparents jumped up and hugged me, telling me how tall I had gotten and how pretty I was. My mother was lying on the couch in a flannel gown with a blanket wrapped around her. Even though she was wrapped up, I could still tell she was very thin. She had dark circles under her eyes, and her lips were chapped.

"Hello, Christie Ann." She was the only person who used both my names.

"Hello, Mother."

We just stared at each other. Daddy finally jumped up and mentioned something about throwing some steaks on the grille. My grandparents said they needed to get home; they had friends coming over to play Bridge. They both kissed my mother, murmured to her in low voices, and hugged me, telling me to be strong; then they left. It was just me and Mama. Even sick, she was still beautiful. She sat up, and the scarf she was wearing around her head slipped down, and I could see she was bald.

"What happened to your hair?"

"I'm taking chemotherapy, and it makes your hair fall out. Could you please hand me that glass of water?"

I handed it to her and took a step back.

"Just because you're dying doesn't mean everything you've done has been forgotten. Not by me anyway."

"I can understand that. I know it's too late for us. I've been a horrible mother. You have every right to hate me."

"I don't need your permission."

She smiled a sad smile.

"I can see you haven't changed a bit. Your daddy said you are in an accelerated English program for writers."

"I don't want to talk to you about my life. It's none of your business."

"You're right; it's not. If you don't mind, I think I am going to rest my eyes for a while." I watched her sleep for a few minutes; then I went to my bedroom and shut the door. I grabbed Lincoln and put my face in his fur. He was so old now, and I knew I wouldn't have him much longer, which broke my heart. I cried and cried until Daddy called me for dinner.

Chapter Twenty-Four

During that summer, I continued working with Dr. Roose and hanging out with my friends. Mother lay on the couch, and Daddy waited on her hand and foot. I just ignored the entire situation. I came home from Missy's house one day in early August, and Daddy told me Lincoln was in a bad way. He said he couldn't hold himself up and he wouldn't eat or drink. I sat down on the floor beside him and tried to get him to eat out of my hand, but he wouldn't even lift his head. Daddy said we needed to take him to see Dr. Roose.

He picked Lincoln up to carry him to the car, and Lincoln yelped. Lincoln was not a dog who yelped. He had almost torn his dewclaw completely off one time chasing a squirrel, and he never even whimpered. I sat in the back seat with him and held his head. I thought about when he was a puppy and how goofy he was, how uncoordinated. I thought about taking him trick or treating with me once and how he stuck his head in a kid's bag, pulling out a candy bar. It seemed like all my memories from the last eight years included Lincoln. He had been my confident and my best friend. I buried my face in his fur and began to cry.

Dr. Roose took him from Daddy when we arrived and disappeared down the hall to the operating room. Dr. Roose loved Lincoln too because Lincoln would go to work with me, and he was such a happy dog; everyone just fell in love with him. About an hour later, Dr. Roose called us into an exam room.

"We did an MRI. He has a large mass on his spine. It's effecting his ability to walk."

"Can you fix him? Isn't there an operation you can do?" I asked.

"Christie, I'm sorry, but I can't. If I was able to remove the mass, his back legs would be paralyzed. He would lose control of his body functions. Honey, he's suffering. I can give him medicine to offset the pain, but that's about it. Christie, you know Lincoln wouldn't want to live this way."

"But you're a doctor. You're supposed to be able to fix it! He will be fine. I just need to take him home and take care of him. I can make him better." I was yelling and crying.

"Christie, I'm so sorry, but it's his time. He's been a very lucky dog to have someone love him as much as you do. Prolonging this will only cause him more pain."

Daddy grabbed my hand. He was crying too.

"Baby, we need to let him go."

"Can I see him?"

"Of course," Dr. Roose said.

He took me to a room in the back. Lincoln was lying on a table with an IV in his paw. There was yellow liquid running down the tube. I walked over to him and buried my face in his fur. I told him how much I loved him. I told him what a great dog he was. I told him I knew he was in pain and he didn't want to leave me, but it was okay to go. I told him he was the best dog in the world, and I would never love another dog as much as I loved him. I thanked him for loving me and being my best friend. I stood there for a long time, sobbing into his neck. I looked into his eyes, and I could see the pain. I told Dr. Roose I was ready to let him go.

Daddy was with him when he died. I couldn't go in the room. When it was over, Dr. Roose wrapped him in the blanket we had brought him in and handed him to Daddy. I held him all the way home. His eyes were closed, and he was so still. I could never remember Lincoln being that still. He even moved his legs when he was asleep. When we got home, Daddy built a wooden box and placed him inside. We put his favorite toy and blanket in with him. Daddy nailed the lid on, dug a hole, and put the box inside. I found a large rock and wrote his name, birth date, and death date. Below that, I wrote, "If love could have saved you, you would have lived forever." I placed the rock at the head of the grave. Daddy and I said the Lord's Prayer, and then he went in the house. I sat by the grave until the stars came out, then I went inside.

Chapter Twenty-Five

School was coming up, and I was going to be a sophomore. In Louisiana, you can drive when you're fifteen. Since I was going to be fifteen in November, Daddy decided I needed a car of my own. He said he was tired of driving me all over hell's creation. I wanted a Plymouth Barracuda, but Daddy bought me a used Lincoln Continental. It was huge! Daddy started taking me out on country roads so I could practice driving it. I was constantly sideswiping things because I couldn't see the rear or sides of the car. I told Daddy I wanted a small car, but he said he wanted something that would protect me if I had a wreck. I started studying for the written part of the exam. It was basically common sense. I wasn't sure why some kids had to take it two or three times before they passed it. My birthday was still three months away, but I was ready.

When I walked up the sidewalk on the first day of school, I thought that it looked sad. It had been built in the 1950s, and there had been no upgrades since. I was taking accelerated English again, but the rest of my schedule was boring with a capital B. I had algebra and biology, and I hated math and science. I was taking a sociology class that sounded interesting. I was also taking World History (snore) and physical education classes because I was on the softball team and we used that time to practice. I thought being a sophomore would make me feel older, but it didn't. Missy had a boyfriend, and that's all she wanted to talk about. We hung out less and less.

I met a girl in my sociology class named Boo. Her real name was Madeline, but for whatever reason, everyone called her Boo. We sat at the same table and soon became big buddies. She was a year ahead of me, so she was already driving. She had a little green Pinto with a white racing stripe. One of the popular things to do in Jena was make loops. You basically drove from one end of town to the other, and if you saw someone you knew, you pulled into the cop shop as we called it and talked to them. The cop shop was the parking lot of the police station. A group of us would get together and find someone to buy us some beer or Boone's Farm Strawberry Hill, and we would head out to the pipeline to drink and act crazy. It was all new to me. At first, I didn't drink, but one night, I took a sip of wine. It didn't taste too bad, so I took another sip; and before I knew it, I had finished an entire cup. I liked the way it made me feel. All the edges were blurry, and the knot I usually had in my stomach disappeared. I felt happy.

The third time I went to the pipeline I noticed a guy sitting on the tailgate of a pickup truck, drinking a beer and telling a story to the people standing around him. Apparently, it was hilarious because everyone was laughing. He was wearing a cowboy hat, a white shirt, jeans, and boots—not cowboy boots but Red Wing boots, the kind of boots people who worked for a living wore. He looked up and caught my eye. He nodded his head and gave me a big smile. He had the whitest teeth I had ever seen. I asked Boo who he was, and she told me his name was Greg. She said he had graduated the year before, and now he worked on an oil rig. I didn't trail after him like a puppy, but I was very aware of where he was all night. It was almost time for me to go. I had an 11:00 p.m. curfew. I set out to find Boo. I walked around the back of one of the parked trucks and ran right into him.

"Whoa there. Where you headed in such a hurry?"

"I, um, I have to, um, have you seen Boo?"

"Yeah, she's riding the three-wheeler with Beau."

"Crap. I need to get home, or I'm going to miss curfew."

"I can take you."

He seemed nice and I loved his smile, but I didn't know him. What if he was another Jake?

"I don't bite, I promise."

"Okay. I live on Carpenter Street. It's about ten minutes from here."

"I know where it is."

I climbed up into his big four-wheel drive truck. It was hard to do gracefully. I finally pulled myself up and in. His truck smelled good—like woodsmoke and something earthy. It was also spotless. We made it back to the main road, and he asked me if I liked Waylon Jennings. I told him my daddy listened to him. I said, "I'm more of a Jim Morrison kind of girl."

He laughed and said, "Well, since I don't own any Doors soundtracks, we will listen to a little Hank Williams."

We had the windows down, and the air was blowing my hair around; the proximity to him and the two plastic cups of wine I'd drunk were making me feel a little dizzy.

"What grade are you in?"

"Tenth. But I started school when I was four, so I'm only fourteen."

He whistled through his teeth. "Jailbait."

"What does that mean?"

"It means I'm nineteen, and if we had sex, you would be considered underage, and I could go to prison for a little something called statutory rape."

I made a note to ask Aunt Dottie about it.

"Well, we aren't going to have sex, so you don't need to worry about going to prison."

About that time, we pulled up in front of my house. I thanked him for the ride and opened my door.

"I'll see you around."

I gave him a little wave and ran into the house. The kitchen was pitch dark, but there was still a light on in the living room. I thought it was probably Daddy waiting up for me, but it was Mama. She was in and out these days. She was hooked up to a morphine drip, so all she had to do was push a button to have the medicine shoot into her veins. She couldn't keep anything down except Campbell's Cream of Chicken soup and lime Jell-O. I stopped at the door.

"Did you have a nice evening?

I wished so much that she was a real mother and that I could tell her I met a boy, and even though I didn't know him very well, I knew he was going to be a big part of my life. But she wasn't a real mother, so I said, "Fine," and walked down the hall to my room. When I took my shirt off, I realized it smelled like the inside of Greg's truck. I laid it on my pillow, put my head down, took a deep breath, and fell asleep.

When I woke the next morning, I knew something was different. I walked quietly down the hall and peeked into the living room. Daddy was sitting on the side of the sofa, holding Mama's hand, and they were talking in low voices. Daddy leaned down and kissed her on the forehead, and when he raised back up, he saw me. "Good morning, Sunshine." For the first time in a long time, I really looked at Daddy. He looked old and very tired. I wondered when that had happened and how I had missed it. He had hired a nurse to help take care of Mama during the day so he could go back to work. After he got home in the evening, he would grab a bite to eat and then sit with her. I realized watching the two of them together how much he loved my mother.

"Hi, Daddy. Do you want me to make you some cheesy eggs?" I asked.

"That would be great, honey. Thank you."

"Mother, can I get you anything?"

Neither one of them spoke for a few seconds; then my mother said, "I would love a glass of orange juice. Thank you."

I was in the kitchen making Daddy's eggs when someone knocked on the back door. I opened it, and Greg was standing there holding my purse. He was much bigger than I remembered. He was at least six foot four and big but not fat. He was barrel-chested as my grandfather would say. I also saw that he had amazing green eyes. I finally stammered out a hello.

"Hi. You left this in my truck last night, and I thought you might need it. I didn't look in it, I swear."

"Thank you for bringing it by. That was really sweet."

We stood there grinning at each other like a couple of idiots.

"Well, here you go." He handed me my purse.

"Great! Thanks again."

"Um, I was wondering, well, a bunch of us are going to Hemps Creek to ride three-wheelers, and I thought you might want to go. Boo is going to be there."

"Um, I'm not sure. I will have to ask my dad. Can you wait just a second?"

I didn't wait for him to answer. I just ran into the living room to ask Daddy. He said no. He said he didn't know Greg and riding three-wheelers was dangerous, and if something happened to me, it would take forever to get me out of the woods and back into town. I begged and pleaded. Finally, Mama said, "Oh, Nick, let her go. She will only be young once, and she has a good head on her shoulders. She will be fine." Daddy insisted on meeting Greg first. When he opened the back door, I could tell he was shocked. There was a giant standing at his door. Greg was very polite and answered all of Daddy's questions. Finally, after what seemed like hours, he agreed to let me go, but I had to be home before dark. Greg said he would make sure of it; then he told me I better put on some blue jeans and rubber boots because the fields were muddy and there were briars. I ran to my room to change.

When I came back into the kitchen, Daddy and Greg were talking like they had known each other for years. Daddy told us to be careful and have fun. We walked out to the driveway, and I climbed back into his big ole truck. It still smelled the same. It smelled like Greg. We didn't talk much. Usually, I talked people's ears off, but I felt shy with him. He was a man, not a boy. He had a job and had probably been around the bases several times. He asked me about school and what my favorite subjects were. I told him the other kids were dissecting frogs in biology, which was my least favorite class, but I had refused to participate on moral grounds. He thought that was hilarious. I told him about my writing class and that we were taking a field trip to Angola prison for our sociology class. We were going to have a tour of death row, and the prisoners were going to make lunch for us.

He told me about working on an oil rig and how dangerous it was. He said he was gone for seven days and home for seven days.

He said he did okay in high school but never considered college. He said he wanted to make money now, not four years from now. He wanted to build a house in the woods and buy and sell cattle. Working on the oil rig was temporary. He said if everything went according to plan, he would have enough money in five years to do what he wanted to do.

Before I knew it, we were at the creek. He parked, and we walked around to the back of his truck and unloaded his three-wheeler. He told me I would be riding behind him. He jumped on the three-wheeler and cranked it. He told me to hop on and put both my arms around his middle and hold on tight. We spent the day riding through the creek and in and out of the woods. He showed me where he wanted to build his house. It was one of the best days I'd had in a long time. Before I knew it, we were loading the three-wheeler back into the truck, heading back to my house. We pulled up in our driveway, and he turned off the engine.

"Man, I wish you were older."

"I'll be fifteen in November."

"You're very mature for your age."

I had heard that my entire life. He looked out the front window and sighed loudly.

"We usually ride every weekend. I'll be at work this coming weekend, but do you want to go the weekend I'm back home?"

"That would be great! I had a lot of fun."

"Okay, I'll call you when I get home. See you later."

I jumped down and ran into the house. I was in love.

Chapter Twenty-Six

Greg and I continued to see each other when he was home. Daddy took him behind the house one day when he was picking me up and talked to him for about forty-five minutes. Neither one of them ever told me what was said. He met Mama and was very sweet with her. She told me he was "a keeper." I don't know if it was because I was truly in love for the first time and I was happy, but I started spending time sitting with Mama. One Sunday afternoon, I was reading *Little Women* to her. It was her favorite book. She was in and out, but on this Sunday, she was having a good day. In the middle of the reading, she said, "I can't go until you forgive me."

I said, "I know you never wanted me. You left me and Daddy, and Daddy suffered for it. I didn't have a mother to do all those things a mother is supposed to do. I hate you for that, and as hard as I try, I just can't let it go."

"I understand. I was a horrible, selfish mother, and I put myself first before you and your Daddy. That was wrong. Christie Ann, I won't lie. I didn't want to have a baby. There were so many things I wanted to do. Did you know I wanted to be a nurse that I graduated with honors and was accepted at LSU?

"No, I didn't."

"Then I met your daddy, and I fell head over heels. I thought I could be married and go to school, but I got pregnant with you right away."

"Yeah, Daddy says you guys were married nine months and fifteen minutes when I was born."

She laughed and rolled her eyes. "That's about right. I got pregnant on our honeymoon. Your dad was so excited; it was hard not to get caught up in his happiness. I still thought I could go to college and be a wife and mother. When you were born, and they put you on my chest, I thought you were the most beautiful thing I had ever seen. I loved you immediately, but I also had a panicked feeling. I felt my dreams slipping further and further away. I had no idea how to take care of a baby. I was so young, only nineteen. I failed miserably. I'm sorry. You deserved so much better. I am so proud of the woman you are becoming. I know you think you are in love with Greg and maybe you are, but, baby, please get your education first. Become a writer. Travel the world. If he really loves you, he will wait. That's enough advice for one day. I'm feeling tired. Could you keep reading to me until I fall asleep?"

"Yes, Mama."

She smiled and closed her eyes. I leaned down to kiss her forehead and whispered in her ear, "I forgive you."

Two days later ~~she~~ passed away. Daddy came into the living room that morning to check on her, and she was gone. He held her body and wailed. I knew I was listening to a heart breaking into a million pieces. I called my grandparents, and they called the funeral home.

The day of her funeral was cool and sunny, her favorite type of day. Fall was her favorite season. The funeral was beautiful. She loved red roses, and I think Daddy bought every red rose in LaSalle Parish. Most of my friends came, and most importantly, Greg came.

After the funeral and the graveside service were over, I stayed in a chair beside her grave. Everyone tried to get me to leave, but I just wanted to sit there for a while longer. I told her all the things I didn't tell her when she was alive. I told her about the homecoming dance and how magical it was. I told her about Diane and about Jake. I told her how angry I had been with her but wasn't anymore. I told her I loved her; then I cried. I cried for the mother she couldn't be. I cried because her dreams didn't come true. I cried because just when I forgave her, she had left me again.

I felt a hand on my shoulder, and when I looked up, it was Greg. He sat down in the chair beside me and grabbed my hand. We sat there in silence until my grandma came to tell us to come and eat. He held my hand all the way to the church. When we walked in, he gave me a little squeeze and let it go. After eating, everyone began to leave.

Daddy and I stood at the door and thanked everyone for coming. When Greg came through the line, he reached down and kissed me on the cheek. He shook Daddy's hand and told him how sorry he was. It was over. The mother I had hated for so long was gone, and I realized how tired I had become from carrying that hate and anger around. I was glad I had forgiven Mama. I was sorry she wouldn't be around when I grew up. I think we would have become friends.

Two weeks later, I turned fifteen. Daddy gave me Mama's pearl ring. He said before she passed, she told him she wanted me to have it for my birthday. I hugged his neck, and we both cried. I put the ring on and knew, like Ernestine's charm bracelet, I would never take it off. My friends bought me eight-track tapes, books, and gag gifts. Greg took me out to dinner and gave me a necklace with a small diamond pendent. He had never kissed me except on the cheek. The only time he held my hand was the day Mama died. I was dying to kiss him, but I understood how dangerous it could be for him. We continued our strange friendship, not calling ourselves a couple, but not dating anyone else either.

One of the stories I wrote about the Vietnam veterans coming home from the war and some of the difficulties they were facing was published in our hometown newspaper and was then picked up by a newspaper in New Orleans. It was a huge honor for me and Daddy, and Greg took me out to dinner to celebrate.

I took and passed my driver's test. I scored 100 percent on the written test. It was nice to be able to drive to school, and my car was so big. It could fit me and five of my friends inside. Daddy was always chastising me for driving too fast, but I felt safe in the "tank" as all my friends called it.

One Saturday night when Greg was offshore, me, Missy, and some of my other friends loaded up and drove to Texaco Town. It was a gas station halfway between Jena and Jonesville, the next down over. The owner didn't ask for IDs. One of my friends was seventeen, so he went in and bought the beer and wine. Everyone was drinking on the way back to town except me. I never drank when I was driving.

We were going down the highway, and I was pushing eighty. All of the sudden, the front left tire dropped off onto the shoulder, and the car started swerving. I slammed on the breaks, which put us into a spin; then the back tires went off onto the shoulder; and the car flipped over once and came to a stop in the middle of the road.

My forehead was bleeding, and everyone was crying and moaning. I looked next to me, and Missy wasn't there. There was a big hole in the windshield. I started screaming her name. We all got out and started looking for her. I found her about twenty yards from the car lying on the side of the road. She was breathing, but her face was all cut up, and her eyes were closed. I bent down and said her name. She didn't respond. I yelled to the others to flag someone down and go get the police and an ambulance. I sat beside her holding her hand, praying she didn't die. The ambulance and police arrived a short time later. I wanted to go in the ambulance with her, but the police said no. They had some questions for me.

They interviewed us one by one. Brad admitted he had bought the beer and wine. This was before there was a tube to blow in, so the police basically made everyone touch their noses and walk a straight line. No one was drunk, and they all told the police that I refused to drink and drive. The EMTs treated all of us for cuts and bruises. I had to have three stitches in my forehead, but I didn't care about that; I just wanted to see Missy.

One of the policemen agreed to take me to the hospital. When we arrived, Missy's entire family and her boyfriend, Sid, were there. I thought they would be mad at me, but they all hugged me and said they were glad I was okay. Missy was awake. She had a concussion, so they wanted to keep her overnight, but she was going to be fine. I asked if I could go in to see her, and the doctor said it was okay for a minute or two. I looked at her mom, and she told me to go ahead.

I walked into the hospital room and saw Missy lying in the bed with a bandage on her head. She looked very pale.

"Hey."

"You are never driving me anywhere again," she said.

We both laughed, and I went over and hugged her around all the tubes. She was released the next afternoon, and both her parents and Daddy gave me a talking to about driving fast. They could have saved their breath. I didn't even want to drive again, much less drive fast. The Lincoln was banged up but salvageable. Daddy put it in the shop, and once it was fixed, he drove it home and parked it under the apple tree in the backyard. I didn't drive it again for six months, and when I did start driving again, I drove very slowly. One of the police officers told Daddy if we had been in a small car, we would all be dead.

Christmas came and went. Daddy and I went to Grandma's with the rest of the family, but it was a quiet affair. Grandma couldn't stand on her feet long enough to cook, so the aunts brought different dishes from home. The food was good, but it just wasn't the same. We were all thinking about Mama, but no one brought her up because we didn't want to upset Daddy. Greg was offshore, so I just hung around the house and read.

One afternoon, I was going through Mama's things Daddy brought back from San Antonio, and I found an old dog-eared copy of *Little Women*. I had started reading it to Mama before she died, but we didn't finish it. I took the book, climbed onto the chair by the window, and began to read.

Chapter Twenty-Seven

Greg was home for New Year's Eve. His parents threw a party for their friends and family every year, and Greg invited me to go with him. His parents' home was beautiful. It was decorated in red and gold. There were funny hats and horns to blow. Greg introduced me to everyone. They all said they were very happy to meet me, and they had heard a lot about me. Halfway through the evening, I excused myself and went to the bathroom. As I was going in, Greg's older sister was coming out. She introduced herself. She looked at me for a long moment and said, "My brother is in love with you. He's dated other girls, but it was nothing like what you and he have. You can see it in his eyes when he looks at you. He cherishes you." I told her I loved him too. She hugged me and went back to the party.

After I came out of the bathroom, I couldn't find Greg. I walked out onto the back porch, and I could hear Greg. His voice was raised. He was talking to his Dad. I stepped back into the shadows so they wouldn't see me.

"You are going to end up in prison."

"No, I'm not! I haven't touched her. We've never even kissed," Greg said.

"She's a child."

"She may be young, but she's more mature than most of the girls I know. She is extremely smart and beautiful, and dammit, Dad, I love her. I'm willing to wait."

"And her? What does she say about all of this?"

"We don't talk about our feelings. We are friends. We like to spend time together. For now, that's enough."

"Son, I'm just worried you may be giving up a chance to settle down, get married, have children."

"Dad, it's my life. I don't want anyone else."

They didn't say anything after that. I quickly turned and went back into the house. It was five minutes until midnight, and I saw Greg come through the door looking for me. I waved, and he gave me that smile that always made my heart flip. He walked over to me, and we started counting down from ten. When everyone said, "Happy New Year," he leaned down and kissed me on the cheek. We looked into each other's eyes, and he said, "I love you, Christie Ann." I didn't tell him that my mother was the only person who called me that. My gaze never left his. "I love you too."

We hugged each other and then laughed and stepped away. I had to be home by twelve thirty, so I went around and told everyone goodbye. Greg drove me home and walked me to the door. He kissed me on the cheek again, and I went inside, yelling to tell Daddy I was home. I went to my room, closed the door, and did a little dance. He loved me; he really loved me.

Chapter Twenty-Eight

There were only two weeks left in the school year. I was busy with softball and my final sociology paper. We had to write a paper about the death penalty: an opposing viewpoint and an assenting viewpoint. I had no problem with the assenting part of the project, but I was having a hard time with the opposing side. I was raised to believe in an eye for an eye. I knew there were bad people in the world. I still remembered the man who had stomped Henry to death. In my opinion, he should have died in the electric chair, not released to hurt more people.

The last Friday before school was out, there was a party on the pipeline. It was the last hoorah before everyone started their summer jobs or went on vacation with their families. Someone had made a couple of coolers full of Hurricanes. The dangerous thing about a Hurricane is you don't taste the liquor. It tastes like Kool-Aid. I was on my fourth glass and was straddling the line between drunk and sick when I heard tires and brakes squealing, and then there was the terrifying sound of metal hitting metal. Everything became eerily quiet and then very loud. We all looked at each other and started running toward the highway.

I heard someone say, "Oh my god," and then girls started screaming, and the boys were telling them to shut up. Someone ran to a house down the road and started beating on the door. I finally pushed my way to the front of the crowd and saw Clint Coleman lying in the middle of the road. One of his legs was bent underneath him, and his head was twisted at a strange angle. His eyes were wide open. There was a black four-wheel drive truck half in and half out of the ditch, and a guy was screaming and crying, "Is he dead? Oh my god, is he dead? I never saw him. He just came out of the side road on his motorcycle. Holy shit. Oh my god. Oh my god." I turned and looked back at Clint. I could see his motorcycle down the road about thirty yards. The front wheel was still spinning.

I backed out of the crowd and went and sat down on a patch of grass a little further down the road. I knew Clint. He was a freshman, but he was smart. He was in my biology class. I remembered when he got the motorcycle. It was in February. His parents gave it to him for his birthday on the condition that he never ride it on the highway. He was a little kid. He was only fourteen years old. He told me one time he wanted to work for the FBI. He was hilarious, and everyone loved him. I couldn't think of one person who disliked Clint. He was just that kind of kid. I saw blue lights from the police cars coming over the hill; then I heard the wail of the ambulance. I walked over to a bush and threw up. It didn't make me feel any better.

Clint's funeral was held three days later. There were so many people; they had to hold it in the school gymnasium. I found out the day after the accident that Clint had been drinking at the party. It was his first high school party. He left because he had to be home for his ten o'clock curfew. He never looked to see if anyone was coming down the road. He hit the highway going fifty miles an hour, hit the truck head-on, and was thrown off the motorcycle. He hit the pavement with his head. He was killed instantly.

I went to the funeral with a group of my friends. After the funeral was over, everyone got in line to speak to his parents. When it was my turn, I told them Clint was in my biology class, how he always finished his assignments first, and then helped other kids who didn't understand the material. I told them he always made me laugh. His mother thanked me, but I could tell by looking in her eyes that she was somewhere else, somewhere extremely painful. Her husband had his arm around her waist, holding her up. She just kept saying, "I never wanted him to have that motorcycle. I never did." She told everyone who talked to her the same thing.

I was only fifteen years old; and I had seen Henry murdered, lost Ernestine, and lost Mama; and now I was looking at a coffin that was holding someone I knew and liked very much. I was beginning to believe God was punishing me or that I attracted death somehow. Maybe it was my penance for hating Mama all those years. All I knew was I had seen enough.

Chapter Twenty-Nine

Greg came home two days after the funeral. When I came home from work, he was at the house. I walked in, and when he saw me, he just held his arms open. I ran to him, and he enfolded me in a hug. I hadn't cried at the scene of the accident or the funeral, but with Greg holding me, I sobbed. By the time I finished, the front of his shirt was soaking wet.

I started talking and couldn't stop. "When I saw him, I kept thinking it must be some awful prank that he was going to jump up and start laughing at how scared we all were. But that didn't happen. He just laid there broken."

"I know, baby. It's okay."

Daddy had been asking me if I wanted to talk about it, and I kept telling him no; but when I started telling Greg what happened, it just poured out of me. I told him about the sickness I felt, about throwing up in the bushes, the horrible taste in the back of my throat, and the smell of blood and burned rubber—the fear and panic that we should all be doing something but not knowing what. How I just wanted to kneel beside him and hold his hand in case, by some miracle, he was still alive. I didn't want him to die alone. But I didn't do anything. I just stood there and looked at him until the ambulance came and took him away.

I told him it all just felt so fucking hopeless. You could do everything you were supposed to do—be a good person, be kind to others, make good grades, follow the rules—and death could still find you. I used to think I could outrun death. I thought I would see it coming for me, and I would outsmart it. I wouldn't let it take me. I would decide my own fate. I didn't believe that anymore.

Chapter Thirty

I started my junior year at Jena High School. Greg and I continued our friendship/relationship. None of my friends believed me when I told them we hadn't even kissed. On the weekends he was home from work, we went riding down country roads, talking about the future, but in a very abstract way. He knew I wanted to get out of Jena as soon as I could and go to college, then New York City. He kidded me about a country boy coming to visit a Yankee city, but we both knew it was just talk. The weeks he was offshore, I either stayed home with Daddy and read or went out with friends.

I had stopped drinking. After what happened to Clint, I just didn't have the desire anymore. There's nothing worse than being sober around people who are drunk, so I went out less and less. Missy and I didn't see each other much; she was always with her boyfriend, Sid, and Boo had started hanging around with a rough crowd that I didn't want any part of.

I was still writing for the Campus Cruiser, but now I was the editor. I was also on the yearbook staff and the softball team. I was more quiet and introspective than I had been and much less tolerant of loud crowds and silly high school drama. The days floated by, and the next time I looked up, it was the first week of November.

My birthday was November 28, and it was going to be my sixteenth. Daddy wanted to throw a big party, but I told him I would rather have a small party with the family. Greg was home that weekend, and I wanted him to meet everyone.

So it was decided Daddy was going to cook burgers and hot dogs, Aunt Dottie was going to make my favorite macaroni salad,

Aunt Elaine was going to bake me a Heavenly Hash cake, and Aunt Bobby was going to make her famous baked beans. I was excited because my aunt Bobby, my uncle Bob, and their daughters, Julie and Lynette, were coming in for my birthday. Aunt Bobby was daddy's older sister, and they lived in Dallas, so we didn't see them much. I had always admired Aunt Bobby. She was extremely smart and was soft-spoken, but you knew when she said something you should listen because it was going to be important. Her daughter Julie was a year older than me, but we were close. She had stayed with us during the summer a few times, and we wrote letters and called each other. Lynette was four years older than me. She was in college, so I didn't know her as well, but she was always nice to me. She never treated me like a little kid.

The big day arrived, and everyone was there. Daddy was playing Mama's Temptations album, and everyone was in a great mood. Greg was there, and he fit right in. After lunch, it was time for presents. Greg was taking me out to dinner that night, so he told me he would give me his present then. I opened my gifts and was thrilled with all of them. Aunt Dottie gave me a book called *The Amityville Horror*, about a family who moved in a haunted house in New York; Aunt Elaine gave me a purple and gold quilt, which were LSU's colors; Aunt Bobby gave me a cashmere sweater that I could tell just from the feel of it was very expensive; and Grandma gave me fifty dollars. I didn't say anything, but there was no gift from Daddy. We were picking up all the wrapping paper when Daddy said, "Oh yeah, I have something for you too. Let me just grab it out of the truck. I didn't have time to wrap it." I told him that was fine.

I was sitting on the couch by Greg when Daddy came in walking backward holding something. I said, "Daddy, what on earth are you doing?"

He turned around and said, "Happy birthday, Sunshine."

I squealed. It was a black Lab puppy with a big red bow around its neck.

"I know how much you miss Lincoln, and even though she will never replace him, I thought she might be fun to have around."

Daddy put her on the floor, and she started chasing her tail. We all laughed. I picked her up and rubbed my face in her fur. She licked me on the nose. She had puppy breath.

Greg said, "Well, what are you going to name her?" He was rubbing her head. I thought for a minute and said, "Scout, after Scout in *To Kill a Mockingbird*."

Everyone thought that was a great name. We all took turns playing with her. I fed her a hamburger. Daddy had forgotten to buy dog food, and she fell asleep in my lap. Everyone left, and I knew I should get ready to go out to dinner with Greg, but I didn't want to leave her. I looked up at him, and he smiled.

"Why don't I pick us up something from Mitchell's, and we can just eat here?" he said.

"Thank you!"

I took Scout to my room and made a pallet for her beside my bed. I wanted to be able to hear her if she needed to go to the bathroom in the middle of the night. Greg went and picked up our dinner, and when he came back, Daddy said he was going over to Grandma's to play a little poker with Uncle Bob. After he left, Greg and I ate our dinner and played with Scout. He pulled a box out of his pocket and handed it to me.

"I know this may seem like a strange gift. I mean, we haven't even kissed, and I know you are going to college after you graduate, but even if it's only for a little while, I want to know you're mine. I love you, Christie Ann."

I took the box and slowly opened it. There was a ring inside with a small diamond in the middle and two diamonds on each side. My eyes filled with tears. He took the ring from my hand and slid it on my right ring finger. It fit perfectly. I leaned over and kissed him on the lips, and he groaned. I pulled back and said, "I love you too." I knew I would never forget my sixteenth birthday.

Greg had to leave the next day to go back to work, but I was happy. Scout kept me busy. Aunt Elaine came over in the morning and walked her, and I would pick her up after school and take her to work with me. I was working for Dr. Roose in the afternoons and on Saturdays too. Everyone at the office fell in love with Scout. It was hard not to. She was such a happy puppy; she reminded me of Lincoln in that way. I took her everywhere with me, and soon everyone in town knew who she was.

Chapter Thirty-One

Things were changing in the world and even though Louisiana was about ten years behind every other state, racism was out in full force. I had occasionally heard people use the *n*-word, but Mama and Daddy didn't allow that word in our house, and they had always supported the civil rights movement, so I really had no idea how bad things were.

One morning, I walked into the square, and there were two groups: one group of black boys and the other group was a bunch of white trash, redneck boys. They were arguing, calling each other names, and then one of the white boys hit one of the black boys with some type of pipe. They all jumped in and started hitting each other. I was frozen. Finally, my friend, Brad Evans, grabbed me and pulled me out of the way. A lot of the kids, both black and white, were cheering them on.

Finally, all the teachers came running out and tried to separate them. Someone called the police, and when they arrived, they couldn't break it up, so they sprayed tear gas at them. Some of it blew in my face, and I started gagging. Someone, I'm not sure who, grabbed me and pulled me into the science building. They took me to the water fountain and made me drink some water. When my head finally cleared, they were gone, but I distinctly remembered the hand on my arm was black.

The police finally broke it up, but there was an undercurrent of fear and hostility running through the school. There were three trees in the square, and the next morning when everyone got to school, there were nooses hanging from all three. The principal came on the intercom during homeroom and said class was dismissed for the day. It was a Friday, so the faculty was hoping things would calm down over the weekend. Greg was offshore, but his mom had called and told him what was going on. He called me that night. I told him about the black hand on my arm leading me out of danger.

"Baby, I know you think all black people are good like Ernestine, but they're not. You were raised different from most people in this part of the country, and I want you to know that there are black people, especially black men, who will hurt you just because you're white. I don't want you going back to JJ's anymore." [JJ's was a catfish place in the quarters where Daddy and I always went to eat.] Promise me, Christie."

I promised and told him I would be careful.

"I'll see you Sunday. Love you."

"I love you too."

When Daddy got home that night, he gave me the same lecture. He said things had shifted and black people were angry. He told me about a group called the Black Panthers and asked me to please not go to the quarters or to any of my black friend's homes. I promised him I wouldn't.

When school was back in session on Monday, there was still an undercurrent of anger. You could feel it simmering below the surface, and everyone was on edge. I was in geometry class when we heard yelling outside the classroom. Mr. Jackson told us to stay seated, and he ran out to the hall. We all ran to the window in the door and looked out. Jeremy Campbell had the best view, and he said five niggers had a white kid on the ground kicking him. There were six teachers and the football coach trying to pull them off. Finally, they separated everyone, and we all ran back and got in our seats. We heard an ambulance siren, and a little later, Mr. Jackson came back into the classroom. His shirt was untucked, and there was blood just above his breast pocket.

"Ladies and gentlemen [he always called us that], there has been an altercation between several of your classmates. Because of the severity of one of the young man's injuries, he has been taken to the hospital in Alexandria. Five more of your classmates have been arrested."

Lee Bradford said, "Who went to the hospital?"

Mr. Jackson said he couldn't tell us because the boy was a minor. The boys started talking about fucking niggers, shooting them, and stringing them up.

"That will be enough! You will not speak that way in this classroom. Now, you are all dismissed until tomorrow morning."

I slowly rose from my desk, grabbed my books, and walked into the hall. You could still see the blood on the floor. The school janitor was trying to mop it up, but he was just smearing it around. Everyone was trying to figure out who went to the hospital. I didn't care. I just wanted to go home and hug Scout. I walked out to the parking lot, got in my car, and laid my head down on the steering wheel.

Laurie Lees, a girl in my history class, knocked on my window. I rolled it down. "The kid they beat up was Scott Williams. They broke his nose, jaw, and several ribs. Keith King said he bet his dad would charge those black boys with attempted murder." Keith King's daddy was the Jena chief of police.

She said, "I know you've always taken up for black people, and I know you had a black nursemaid or something when you were little, but doing that now will get you killed. You better be careful."

I thanked her for telling me. I didn't know Scott very well. We didn't have any classes together, but I knew he didn't try to hide the fact that he didn't like black people. Rumor was he was one of the kids who hung the nooses in the tree.

I left school and went to Daddy's office to tell him what happened. I knew he would be worried about me if he heard it from someone else. We sat and talked quietly with the door closed. Daddy already knew about it. One of the women who worked in his office was married to one of the town's police officers.

"Daddy, is it ever going to get better? It seems like this fight has been raging since the civil war."

"I don't know, honey. I honestly don't know. I think you should go stay with Uncle Bob and Aunt Bobby for a while until all this blows over."

I didn't want to go to Dallas. My life was in Jena, good or bad. There was no way I was leaving my school, my friends, my job, Greg, or Scout. I was going to tough it out. Daddy said we would wait and see what happened with the boys who were arrested.

We found out later that day that one of the boys was Ernestine's grandson. He was her daughter Felecia's son. That made sense to me because Felecia had fought so hard for equal rights and had spent several years in Mississippi when black people were being hosed and attacked by dogs. His name was Willie Purvis. He was in my accelerated English class. He was a great writer. I had known him since I was six. He always spoke to me in the hall and waved at me when we saw each other in town. He was a nice boy. I couldn't believe he would hurt someone the way Scott had been hurt.

I didn't tell Daddy, but when I got home, I called Ms. Felecia to see how Willie was doing. She told me we were at war, and I needed to decide which side I was on. I told her I didn't want to be on either side. I just wanted everyone to get along. She told me to watch out for myself and hung up. I desperately wished Ernestine was alive so I could talk to her. She would know what to do.

Chapter Thirty-Two

When I arrived at school the next morning, the National Guard was there. They had guns and were stationed at the end of each hall and outside in the square. Everyone was very quiet. Greg was home from work, and he took me to school and picked me up. He took me to work, softball practice, and anywhere else I needed to go. When he was at work, Daddy took me. There were black girls on the softball team with me, and I had always considered them my friends. Now they wouldn't even look at me or talk to me. It broke my heart. What was the point of the civil rights movement? What about all those people, black and white, who gave their lives to make things better? It was worse now than it had ever been.

The five boys who beat up Scott were charged with attempted murder just like Keith said they would be. All of a sudden, Jena was very popular. There were people there from news stations as far away as New Orleans and Houston. They tried to talk to us, but the National Guardsmen kept them back. The *New York Times* called us the most racist city in America.

The five boys who were involved in the attack on Scott were now being called the Jena Five. The trial was coming up, and there were television reporters staked out in front of the courthouse. Daddy wouldn't let me go to the trial. We got our updates from the evening news. Willie was being tried as an adult because he had a prior record. His record included shooting off fireworks in town and trespassing on someone's property.

Scott testified. Missy went to the trial every day, and she would call me at night and give me an update. Her uncle was a police officer, so he was able to get her in. She told me when Scott testified, you could hardly understand him because his jaw was still wired shut. She said none of the five boys took the stand. Their attorney who was court-appointed and white. All five boys were found guilty and given sentences ranging from fifteen years to life in prison. Because Willie was thought to be the ringleader and was tried as an adult, he was given a life sentence with the possibility of parole after twenty-five years. He would be forty-one years old when he got out, half of his life gone. When I heard the news, I was in shock. The Willie I saw on television was not the Willie I had known most of my life. I was glad Ernestine wasn't there to see it.

Nothing had changed, and I honestly believed it never would. Fifteen thousand people from all over America descended on Jena and protested the verdicts. They left after several days, and things slowly went back to normal. Black kids sat on one side of the square, and the white kids sat on the other. We didn't speak to each other in the halls. There was no more kidding around in the locker room after softball practice. We pretty much ignored each other. The school year ended, and I was glad. I was officially a senior. I couldn't wait until the next year was over so I could leave Jena forever.

Chapter Thirty-Three

School ended, and I continued working for Dr. Roose. I went to a creative writing camp at LSU for two weeks. It was amazing. The camp was from 9:00 a.m. to 1:00 p.m. each day, and then you were on your own for the rest of the day. I walked the entire campus. I felt at home there, like everything I had ever dreamed of was finally in sight. The dream I had carried since I was six years old was going to become a reality. I missed Daddy, Greg, and Scout, but being this far away from home didn't bother me as much as I thought it would. Jena seemed very far away. I was ready to begin the next phase of my life, but first I needed to get through my senior year.

When I came back from Baton Rouge, Greg and I resumed our relationship. I spent the summer like the summers before, hanging out with friends, going to the creek, riding three-wheelers with Greg, and working. Even though I enjoyed all those things, I felt removed from them at the same time. Going to LSU had given me a new perspective. The writing camp was the first time I was around other kids like me, kids who saw the world a little differently and who could turn even the most mundane situation into a story. It was wonderful to share ideas and have someone give you an honest opinion about your work. It was exhilarating and terrifying at the same time.

School started again, and because I had taken most of the credits I needed to graduate, I finished at eleven forty each day. I didn't have to be at work until three o'clock, so Scout and I went to the creek quite a bit; she was a typical Lab and liked to swim. We walked in the woods, and I kept finding myself at the spot where Greg wanted to build his house. He had purchased the land several months before. It felt bittersweet. I knew in my heart as much as I loved him, it was temporary. Our goals were too different. I couldn't imagine living in Jena for the rest of my life, and he couldn't imagine living anywhere else.

Summer turned to fall, and my seventeenth birthday rolled around. Greg and I didn't talk about it, but we were both aware that things had shifted. I was legally an adult. Finally, on Valentine's Day, he brought it up. We had just finished dinner and were riding around on the backroads talking. We could talk for hours about everything and nothing. He knew all my thoughts and dreams. I trusted him above all others. We parked near the creek, and I scooted over to sit beside him.

"Well, you are officially an adult."

"I am."

"Christie, I'm not going to beat around the bush here. I've waited three years to do this."

He leaned over and softly kissed me. It was everything I had imagined it would be. It was soft and tender and extremely sweet, just like him. We continued kissing, and the kisses became deeper and more urgent. Finally, Greg pulled away.

"Good god, woman. You're killing me."

"I'm sorry. Should we stop?"

"Yes, but not because I want to. Christie, I want to be close to you and love you. Do you understand what I'm saying?"

I told him I did. I told him I didn't want my first time to be in the cab of a truck. We hatched a plan to tell Daddy I was spending the night with Missy the next weekend, but instead Greg and I were going to go to Alexandria to spend the night in a hotel. I was terrified, but I knew this was what I wanted to do. I knew Greg loved me and I loved him. I knew he would never hurt me.

I told Missy the plan, and she agreed to go along with it. She was happy for me and said, "Finally! I was beginning to think you were going to be an old maid. Let's go shopping for lingerie."

We drove to Alexandria and went to a store Missy frequented when she needed something special. I was embarrassed just being in the store. I knew there was no way I could wear those things in front of Greg. We finally found a white silk nightgown that landed just above my knee. I knew it was the one. I took it home and hid it in the back of my closet. Missy told me I needed to go to the health center and get birth control. I went after school on Monday, but the nurse who examined me said it took a week for it to work. I only had five days. I told Greg, and he said he would take care of that part of it.

Saturday arrived, and I went to Missy's to get the lowdown on how exactly things worked and what I was expected to do. She and Sid had been having sex for two years. Some of the things she told me sounded disgusting. I knew I could never do that. That night, Missy took me to town to meet Greg. I was wearing a dress and heels. When he saw me, he said I looked beautiful. He came around to my side of the truck and put the little stool he had for me on the ground and helped me climb into the truck. I waved goodbye to Missy, and we took off. I was about to become a woman.

We arrived at the hotel, and Greg paid for our room. I had my little overnight bag with my new outfit inside. My hands were shaking, and I felt like I was going to throw up.

When we walked into the room, Greg took my hand and we sat down on the bed.

"You don't have to do this," he said. "I will love you no matter what."

I told him I would be right back. I took my bag into the bathroom and put my gown on. I opened the door and walked into the room. I heard his breath catch.

"Oh, baby. You are so beautiful. What on earth do you see in me?"

I walked over to him, and he stood; I had to stand on my tiptoes to wrap my arms around his neck. We took our time. He kept telling me how much he loved and adored me. There was pain involved, but I expected that. Missy had told me all about it. When it was over, we both cried and held on to each other. We fell asleep, and when we awoke, we tried it again. This time, there was no pain, and I finally understood what all the fuss was about.

We ordered room service. Friends of mine who had lost their virginity told me I would feel different, older when it finally happened. I didn't have that feeling. Aunt Dottie always said I was an old soul. All I knew was, I had felt old as long as I could remember. We spent the night in each other's arms, and the next morning, we made love again. It was urgent as if we both knew we only had a certain amount of time together and we had to make the most of it. We left Alexandra around eleven and headed for Jena. We kept looking at each other and smiling. Everything had been perfect.

Chapter Thirty-Four

The end of school was right around the corner, and I was heading to LSU in June to begin a writing class for high school students who had been in accelerated English. There was a lengthy application process to determine if you were good enough to be in the class. Either someone screwed up, or I really could write because I made the cut. There was a visiting author who was teaching the class, and I was excited to get started. I would be staying in a dorm and would finish the class right before the fall semester began. Greg promised to come visit, but we both knew our great love affair was winding down.

I was extremely busy with softball and finishing up the yearbook. I had resigned from the veterinarian's office in March. I wanted to enjoy the last couple of months of my senior year. The staff threw a party for me and gave me a bunch of gifts I could use in college. Dr. Roose gave me a beautiful leather messenger's bag. He said he heard writers in New York City carried bags just like it. He hugged me hard and told me not to be a stranger. I made it to my car before the tears came. I knew I would miss the animals and the staff, but it was time. I told myself I would visit when I came home for the holidays.

Graduation day arrived, and my entire family was there. I missed Mama and wished she could see me, but I knew she and Ernestine were looking down from heaven. I won a scholarship from the newspaper for a thousand dollars. When I went up on stage to accept the check, my family yelled and screamed. It was embarrassing but very sweet. After graduation, I went to my last party on the pipeline. I went around and talked to everyone telling them goodbye. Only 10 percent of my graduating class would be attending college.

Most of the boys were going to work offshore, and the girls were planning weddings. I couldn't understand how they could be content with such mediocre lives.

The night before I left for my summer class, Greg and I went to his land. He took a blanket out of the truck, and we lay on it looking at the stars. We talked about all the things we had been through together, how special our relationship was, and how we would never forget each other. We made love one last time, and it was very slow and heartbreakingly sweet. I told him I would always love him. We lay there and held each other for a long time. The next morning, I headed to Baton Rouge.

Chapter Thirty-Five

The writing class was demanding but in a good way. I made friends with several of the other kids in the class. They called me "Pulitzer" because the instructor was always reading my stories and telling the class, "This is how you develop a character. This is how you describe an experience." It made me feel good when they called me that, but everyone in the group was good. I learned a tremendous amount about content and character and maintaining a balance between comedy and drama. I learned how important research is especially in nonfiction books. I felt like I was exactly where I was supposed to be as I took it all in.

The third weekend in July when I had been there a little over six weeks, I started feeling sick. I couldn't keep any food down, and the smell of anything fried made me nauseated, which, if you have ever been to Louisiana, you know everything is fried. I was living off soft-serve vanilla ice cream. I assumed I had the stomach flu and it would be over in a few days. When July turned to August and I was still sick, I went to the infirmary. Even though I was eating ice cream constantly, I knew I was losing weight. My clothes were hanging off me.

I walked into the clinic and gave the receptionist my name. She gave me a stack of paperwork to fill out, and once that was finally done, a nurse took me back to an exam room. The doctor walked in and shook my hand. He didn't look much older than me. He checked my ears and throat and felt around on my stomach. He sat down on his rolling stool and asked me when my last period was. I felt bile in the back of my throat. My periods had always been irregular, and I had been so busy with the writing class; I hadn't really given it much thought. I started counting backward and realized my last period had been at the end of May.

I told him the dates, and he asked me if I had been sexually active since then. I told him only once at the beginning of June. I started thinking about the last night Greg and I were together. I didn't remember hearing the rip of the condom package, but I assumed he took care of it. I told all of this to the doctor. He sent me to the bathroom for a urine sample. I gave it to the nurse, and she took me back to the exam room. The doctor came in a few minutes later.

"Christie, according to the urine sample, you're pregnant. I need to do an exam to determine how far along you are." He stepped out of the room, and the nurse came back in. She handed me a paper gown and told me to take everything off from the waist down and put the gown on. I felt like I was moving through molasses. It was almost an out-of-body experience. I changed, climbed up on the table, and waited for the doctor. He came in and told me to scoot down and put my feet in the stirrups. A couple of minutes later, he told me I could sit up.

"It looks like you're about six weeks along. I take it this wasn't planned."

"No, it wasn't."

"There are options you can talk to our counselor about. Are you still in contact with the father?"

"We've spoken a couple of times on the phone, but I haven't seen him since June."

"Okay, once you're dressed, walk down to the counselor's office at the end of the hall. She will give you some information to help you decide next steps. The nurse will give you a prescription for the nausea. I would like to see you back in a month."

I got dressed and walked down the hall. I knocked on the door that said counselor on it and a tired-sounding voice told me to come in. I walked in, and a tiny little woman about sixty years old was sitting behind a large desk. *Roe v. Wade* had just passed the United States Supreme Court making abortions legal, but that didn't mean women in Louisiana were having them. Louisiana was a very conservative state, and I didn't know any girls I went to high school with who had an abortion. It was murder, plain and simple. I could not imagine killing a baby. The counselor talked to me about keeping the baby and raising it myself, putting it up for adoption, or, as a last resort, an abortion. She said the only place to obtain an abortion was in New Orleans or Houston, and they cost a thousand dollars or more. I told her I needed some time to process everything. She gave me some pamphlets and said she was there each day until five o'clock if I had any questions.

I walked back to my dorm room in a daze. Pregnant? That changed everything. I saw all my plans slipping away. I knew if I told Greg, he would want to marry me. I would end up like all those girls in high school who got pregnant and then married instead of the reverse order like it should be. I always felt superior to those girls. I knew that would never happen to me because I was too smart. I was going to be a famous writer, live in an apartment in New York City, and hang out with other famous writers. This was not how my story was supposed to end. My friends from the class were going barhopping that night, and they said they had a fake ID I could use. I told them I was just going to go to bed and read. I told them I was still under the weather.

I looked through all the pamphlets. I knew Greg would never sign his rights away so the baby could be adopted. I also knew if I had an abortion and he found out, he would never forgive me. He wanted kids. We had talked about it several times. He said he wanted at least three, two boys and a girl. I made it very clear to him and everyone else that I never wanted kids. I didn't even like kids. I had never babysat any kids. I had no idea what you were supposed to do with them. My mind was racing a hundred miles a minute. The only person I could think of to call was Diane. I hadn't talked to her in a couple of years, but I knew if anyone would know what I should do, it would be her.

I went to the communal phone in the hall. School was out for the summer, so the only people around were the kids from my writing class, and they were at the bar. I still knew Diane's number by heart. She answered on the third ring.

"Hello?"

"Diane?"

"Oh my god! Christie, is that you?"

I said yes, and then I started crying.

"Oh no. Sweetie, what's wrong? Are you hurt? Has something happened to your dad?"

I was crying so hard; I couldn't talk. I finally choked out the word pregnant.

"Oh no, Christie, oh no. How far along?"

I stopped crying long enough to tell her about my visit to the clinic.

"I'm leaving now. I will be there in about four hours. Are you sharing a room with anyone?"

"No, I have my own room."

"What dorm are you in?"

"Acadian Hall."

"I'm on my way; just hold on. We will figure this out."

I hung up the phone and walked back to my room. Diane found me there four hours later curled into a ball. She took me in her arms and rocked me, telling me over and over that everything was going to be okay. I desperately wanted to believe her.

That night, Diane slept in my room in the other bed. I woke up off and on all night, and each time I opened my eyes, the news hit me again full force. What would Daddy think? What would my family think? I was the first person in our family to go to college. How could I let everyone down?

The next morning, Diane and I talked about my options. We spent the day going back and forth. For me to achieve my dream, I would have to either put the baby up for adoption or have an abortion. I knew Greg would never allow me to give our baby up to be raised by strangers. After weighing all my options, I decided an abortion was the best decision. I cried and cried, but the alternative was not an option. I didn't want to be married and have a baby at the age of seventeen. Diane called a clinic in New Orleans, but they couldn't perform the procedure until Thursday morning, which was three days away.

Over the next three days, I must have changed my mind a hundred times. I went to class, but I don't remember anything we discussed. Diane stayed the entire time. The night before I was supposed to have the abortion, I was lying in bed, and I felt something wet between my legs. I pulled back the sheet, and there was blood everywhere. I woke Diane up, and she helped me put a towel between my legs, dressed me, and rushed me to the emergency room. The nurse took me back immediately. Diane told them she was my mother so they would let her go back with me. The doctor said I was having a miscarriage and I was hemorrhaging. They had to take me into surgery to do a D&C. Once I was in the operating room, they put a mask over my face, and the next thing I remembered I was waking up in a hospital room. Diane was dozing in a chair beside the bed.

The doctor walked into the room, and Diane jerked awake.

"Hi, Christie. How are you feeling?"

"Empty."

"You had a miscarriage, and we went in and performed a D&C. In layman's term, we scraped the excess tissue out of your uterus to stop the bleeding. You will bleed for several days, and you can't have intercourse for six weeks; but other than that, you should be fine."

I thanked him. I looked over at Diane, and we both started crying. I didn't want the baby, but I didn't want it scraped out of my uterus either. I was so relieved there would be no abortion. I wasn't sure I would have been able to go through with it. I didn't know the baby long enough for it to become a reality, but I stilled mourned for it. Was it a boy or girl? Did it have Greg's eyes and sweet smile? Would it have been able to write stories and play softball? I would never have answers to those questions and that made me extremely sad.

Diane stayed another day and then went back to Houston. While she was with me, I told her about Jake. She said she was sorry I had carried that around for all those years. She had suspected something happened between us but wasn't sure what it was. She said she wished I had told her. She told me she dumped him right after I left. Apparently, he had tried to stick his tongue down one of her friend's throats, and her friend kneed him in the nuts and then told Diane. We talked about whether I should tell Greg about the baby, and we both agreed it would be better if he never knew. There was nothing to be gained from what might have been.

Chapter Thirty-Six

I went home for a week before I officially started my freshman year at LSU. I enjoyed seeing everyone, but it seemed like everyone was still swimming around in a pond and I had jumped feet first into the ocean. Greg was offshore that week, so I didn't get to see him. In a way I was glad, I didn't think I could have stayed quiet about the baby. I went over to see Missy; there were a lot of empty spots in our conversation. She was planning her wedding to Sid and asked me to be the maid of honor. I told her I would love to. We talked about venues and colors, and I left after an hour or so. I told her I would make sure I was back for the wedding, and I would take care of the bachelorette party.

I dropped by Cleda's Flower Shop and bought two bouquets of flowers. One was red roses, and the other was tulips, Ernestine's favorite flower. I went to Mama's grave and put the roses in the vase that was attached to her headstone. I told her all about my writing class and how excited I was about starting college. I told her about the baby. I told her I wished she was still here so she could see how much of her was in me. I told her I loved her.

After visiting Mama, I went to the cemetery in the quarters to say goodbye to Ernestine. I told her how much I missed her and loved her. I told her I was the person I was in large part because of the way she had raised me. I thanked her for being a mother to me. I laid the flowers on her grave and walked back to my car.

Daddy had replaced the "tank" with a Plymouth Valiant. He gave it to me when I graduated from high school. I loved it, but I missed the Lincoln.

Scout was doing great—fat and happy. She loved me, but she was more Daddy's dog now. He took her to work with him every day, and she followed him everywhere. Daddy was dating Dr. Turnley's nurse, Kathy. I was happy for him. I had known Kathy my entire life. She was a nice lady. She had two daughters, Michelle and Kim. I thought it would be nice if she and Daddy married so I could finally have siblings. I saw my grandparents, my aunts, my uncles, and my cousins. The week flew by, and I was loading my car when Daddy walked out and handed me a small box.

"Daddy, you've done enough. You didn't have to get me anything."

"I know. I just wanted to make sure you don't forget your old daddy when you become a famous writer."

I hugged him and told him that would never happen. I opened the box, and inside was a beautiful gold sun on a thin chain.

"Turn it over."

I was crying as I flipped it over. Engraved on the back, it said, "You are my sunshine." I suddenly had a memory of being small and sick and Daddy singing to me, "You are my sunshine, my only sunshine." How could I have forgotten that?

I hugged Daddy hard and told him how lucky I was that he was my dad. I told him I would call him every week.

"You don't worry about me. You go out and make your mark in the world, baby girl. It's your time now."

I thanked him for everything.

"I love you, Daddy."

"I love you too, Sunshine. Always have, always will."

We smiled at each other, and I got in my car and headed south, leaving Jena in the rearview mirror.

Chapter Thirty-Seven

I arrived in Baton Rouge during the hottest part of the afternoon and hauled all my things into my dorm room. I didn't know my roommate. None of my friends were going to LSU, so I told the college to just choose someone for me. When I walked in the room, one side was already done. The bed was made up with a rainbow bedspread. There was a bulletin board hanging over the bed with pictures thumbtacked to it. I opened the top dresser drawer, and there were stacks of clothes folded neatly inside. When I looked in the closet, shoes were lined up in rows. I was so glad she wasn't a slob because I was extremely organized and liked everything in its place.

The door to the room flew open, and a girl with bright-red curly hair walked in holding two sandwiches and two Cokes.

"You must be Christie. I'm Amy. It's nice to meet you."

"You too."

"So I wasn't sure if you would be hungry, but I bought you a sandwich and a Coke. I hope you like turkey."

I told her turkey was fine and thanked her for buying it for me. I tried to pay her back, but she said no. She said I could get the next one.

She helped me make up my bed. I had brought the quilt Aunt Elaine made me that was LSU colors, purple and gold. I put my clothes and shoes away. We decided to pool our makeup and share the vanity. I hung a poster showing the cover of *To Kill a Mockingbird* over my bed. We grabbed our sandwiches and sat cross-legged on our beds facing each other. Amy told me her parents were divorced, and she had one brother, Jason, who was two years older than her and in the marines. She said she was close to her mom but never really saw her dad. She was from Shreveport and had a boyfriend there, but it was nothing serious. She was a journalism major, so we would both be writing, except I would be writing books and she would be writing newspaper articles. I liked her and thought we would get along well and hopefully become friends.

I was in the English Honors program. My classes for the first semester were the following: English 2823 Honors: Studies in Literary Traditions and Themes; English 2824 Honors: Critical Analysis of Literature and Discourse; Statistics; and Abnormal Psychology. I wasn't sure why I needed Statistics to get a creative writing degree, but it was a prerequisite. It was the only class I didn't like.

Amy and I spent most of our free time together. We both agreed sororities were lame. All those girls wore pencil skirts, sweater sets, and pearls. None of them had an original thought in their heads. Amy said they were there to get an MRS degree not to become rich and famous like us. The semester moved quickly, and before I knew it, the Christmas holidays had arrived. Amy invited me to Shreveport to spend Christmas with her and her family, but I wanted to be with Daddy. He and I spoke every Sunday night, and he kept me up to date on all the gossip. Missy's wedding was coming up in February, but she had called and asked if I minded if Sid's sister was the maid of honor. They had become close. I told her it was fine, and it was. I knew Greg was going to be at the wedding, and I was reluctant to see him. I still loved him, but I knew that he would never fit into my world or I in his. He sent me a letter with a picture of his land. All the trees had been cleared, and he was ready to begin building his house. I was happy for him.

Christmas with the family was great, but when the holiday was over, I was ready to get back to school. For my second semester, I was taking three English classes and a sociology class. I had enjoyed the sociology class I took in high school and looked forward to learning more about the problems we faced as a society in a college class. Our professor asked us to write a paper on what we perceived to be the most pressing issue we currently faced as a society. I wrote about racism in America and how prevalent it still was, especially in the

South. I received an A on the paper, and because my professor was good friends with Morris Dees, I also received an invitation to read my paper at the Southern Poverty Law Center's annual conference in June.

My sociology professor talked to me about becoming a civil rights attorney instead of a writer, but I told him it had always been my dream to become a writer, and I couldn't imagine doing anything else. He asked me to take his Intro to Criminal Law class my sophomore year just to "dip my toes in the water." I told him I would think about it.

I attended the SPLC conference in June, and one morning, I found myself alone in the elevator with Morris Dees. He was reading a document, so I discreetly coughed into my hand. When he looked up, I told him I was a great admirer of his and all the work he had done with regard to civil rights. He said he had read my paper, and he was a great admirer of mine. He also suggested I consider law as my major. I told him I was thinking about it.

I was scheduled to read my paper during the closing ceremony. I was both nervous and excited. When the time came, I read my paper without stuttering or stumbling over the words. I had read it so many times; I knew it by heart. There were over two thousand people in the audience, and they gave me a resounding round of applause. It was one of the top ten best moments of my life, so far. I went back to LSU to begin my summer internship at the Louisiana State University Press. I mainly made coffee and mimeographed documents for the staff, but I learned about the book publishing process and made some good contacts.

I went home for a week before classes started and went by to see Missy. She was pregnant. She and Sid were both so happy and were busy working on the nursery. I took a mobile that had little cotton books attached to it to hang over the baby's bed. They loved it and said they hoped the baby would like to read as much as I did. While Missy and I were sitting out on the porch, drinking sweet tea, and gossiping, she told me Greg was getting married in October. I felt like I had been sucker punched. I knew the girl he was engaged to. She was sweet and pretty, and I knew she probably worshipped him.

I told Missy that was great news. I told her I was happy for him. I left soon after.

I don't know what I had expected. I guess I was holding on to some small hope that one day we would end up back together. I figured we would split our time between New York City and Jena. There were boys at LSU who asked me out, but none of them interested me. I compared them all to Greg, and so far, none of them had measured up. I rode out to the creek. There were a bunch of teenagers riding three-wheelers and having a blast. I sat there until the sun began to go down, thinking of all the memories I had and how most of those memories included Greg. I knew it was time to let him go. My heart ached, and I knew I would never love another man as much as I had loved him. He was my first in every way.

Chapter Thirty-Eight

During the middle of my sophomore year, I began to date a guy who played on the basketball team, Scott. His family owned Kleinpeter Dairy, which supplied all the dairy products to south Louisiana. His parents lived in a beautiful antebellum home in Baton Rouge near the college. The house had been in their family since Sherman marched on Atlanta. It had barely survived the civil war, and every time I went over there, I had to hear about those damn Yankees burning the cotton and taking everything worth anything out of the house when they left. Apparently, that group of Yankees weren't particularly bright because the fire they set burned itself out.

Scott's great-great-great-grandfather brought the house back to its original glory, and other than some minor changes and updated conveniences, the house looked exactly like it did in 1864. Scott's family was very prim and proper, and they had no idea what to make of me. His mother was involved in charitable activities and loved to have lady's luncheons. I always had somewhere else I needed to be when it was time for one of those. His sister was in the junior league and wore pearls with everything. She and I had absolutely nothing in common. His brother was a senior at LSU. He was majoring in chemical engineering. I had only met him once. He was dating some debutante from New Orleans. Scott's parents were thrilled.

Thanksgiving came around, and Scott invited me to his family's home for dinner. Daddy and Kathy had married the summer before, and they were taking a trip to Iowa to visit her daughter Michelle and her family for Thanksgiving, so I was on my own. Amy invited me to go home with her; she and I were still roomies except now we lived in an apartment on campus, but she was staying the entire week, and I didn't want to do that. She was dating one of Scott's friends, Daniel. I couldn't think of any reason not to go to Scott's parents, so I agreed.

Scott picked me up Thanksgiving morning, and we drove to his parents' house. I was nervous, and that made me angry. I was raised to believe I was just as good as anyone else, if not better, and I didn't like the way Scott's mother and sister made me feel—like I was less than. I had worn a dress for the occasion but no pearls. I did trade my field jacket and cowboy boots for a sweater and high heels. I was uncomfortable and grouchy. Scott and I argued on the way there about something completely inconsequential. We pulled up in front of the house, and Nelson came and opened my door. That was another thing that bothered me about his family. They still had servants. Going over there was like being in a damn stage production of *Gone with the Wind*.

Scott's parents met us at the door. His mother kissed me on both cheeks and told me how lovely I looked. She led us into the sitting room with the rest of the family. The women were having gin and tonics, and the men were having brandy. When Luella asked what I would like to drink, I asked for a brandy on the rocks. You could have heard a pin drop.

"Well, Christie, I didn't know you were a brandy drinker," Mrs. Kleinpeter said.

"Usually, I'm not, but I don't like gin."

"Well, that's fine then."

I said, "Thank you."

Who did these people think they were? I didn't need their permission to drink brandy or anything else for that matter. Maybe for dinner I would ask if they had any hooch in the back of the cabinet. There was wine with dinner, which was five courses, and went on forever. Scott's brother, DeWayne, asked me what I was going to do with a creative writing degree. His tone was sarcastic. I told him I planned to write the next great American novel. I told him I wanted to write a book that made a difference, like *To Kill a Mockingbird*. He said, "You know Harper Lee's a lesbian, right?" He was slurring his words, and it dawned on me that he was extremely drunk. They all were. I said, "How do you know that DeWayne? She turn you down?"

"Hell no. I read it somewhere."

"Where? At the back of a *Playboy* magazine?"

I looked at Scott and said, "I'm ready to go."

Mr. Kleinpeter asked me to please stay and ignore DeWayne. He was a rude drunk. I stood up and placed my napkin on the table, thanked Scott's parents for inviting me, and started walking toward the door. If Scott wasn't going to take me home, I would catch the bus. He caught me halfway down the driveway.

"Christie, wait! I'll drive you back. Just come back and get in the truck."

I told him to go get the truck and pick me up. He ran back up the hill and drove down, and I climbed in the truck. Halfway back to my apartment, he started laughing, and then I did too.

"Did you see Dewayne's face? No woman has ever talked to him like that."

"Well then, it was about time. He's an ass."

We drove up to the front of my apartment, and I leaned over to kiss Scott goodbye. He grabbed my hand, pulled me back, and kissed me on the lips.

"Are we ever going to have sex?" he asked.

"Well, don't beat around the bush, Scott. Just go ahead and say what you're thinking."

"We've been dating three months. I've never waited this long."

"Thank you for your sacrifice but trust me, you don't need to do me any favors."

"It's that guy from your hometown, isn't it? That Greg guy?"

I jumped out of the truck. "Good night, Scott." I walked into my apartment. I knew I wouldn't hear from Scott again, and I was okay with that. We were very different people, and I had no desire to live in his world. He would marry some cheerleader his parents would approve of, and they would all live happily ever after. I wasn't that girl.

Chapter Thirty-Nine

My sophomore year came to an end, and I was shocked when three weeks before the semester ended, Morris Dees called me from Atlanta to offer me an internship at the law center. He said he had heard through the grapevine that I took an Intro to Criminal Law and a Civil Rights Law class during the fall semester. I told him I did, but I didn't believe that qualified me to intern at the law center. He said he had been keeping tabs on the stories I was writing for both the LSU newspaper and the Baton Rouge *Advocate*. He said he didn't want me to intern in a legal capacity. He wanted me to work in the public relations department, writing editorials about racism and sexism. I asked him to give me a few days to think about it. He told me it was a paid internship, and I could stay with him and his wife while I was in Atlanta.

I had written a five-part series about the Jena Five and where the boys who had been involved were now. Two of the five had been paroled and were in college. Two others were up for parole in three years, and Willie was still in for life. He wouldn't be up for parole for another twenty-one years. I included information that had not been made public during the trial. I spoke to all five of the boys, saving Willie for last.

I went to Angola prison to interview Willie for the series. I smiled when he walked in and sat down, but his face showed no emotion. We were separated by glass, and I could see how prison had aged him. The little boy who used to pull my ponytail and run away laughing had been replaced by a hardened man with hate in his eyes.

He picked up the phone and gestured for me to do the same. I told him what I was doing.

"Why you wanna do that?" he asked.

Even his speech had changed. Willie had always been well-spoken and extremely articulate, but now he spoke like one of the Black Panthers I saw on television all the time. They were always raging about something.

"Because I think you got a raw deal. You were no more or less guilty than the other four."

"Yeah, well, the jury thought different," he said.

"Did you tell those boys to hurt Scott Williams?" I asked.

He stared at me for a long moment trying to determine if I was trustworthy. I thought he was going to tell me the truth, but then the hood dropped back over his eyes, and he laughed a harsh, ugly laugh.

"You always acted like you was one of us because of my grandma. You went to our church, you ate at our restaurants, I even remember you coming to grandma's house when that cracker stomped Henry to death, but what you needs to get through yo head is, you just another cracker looking at us from the outside. You want to be one of us? Paint yo ass black and drive around that college you go to. See how many times you get called nigger and how many times the police pull you over. Then you might know what it's really like to be one of us. I got nothing to say to you. Guard!"

The guard came over and handcuffed Willie behind his back. I sat and looked at him with tears in my eyes. Before the guard closed the door, Willie turned around and looked at me.

"I'm a lost cause, Christie. Use your life on something better than trying to help me. I'm already dead."

I didn't remember leaving the prison or walking to my car. The next thing I knew, I was driving back to Baton Rouge. I didn't believe Willie. I knew he wanted out of that place. I drove straight through to Jena and went to the newspaper office. The editor, Mr. Sammy Franklin, had known me since we moved to Jena when I was twelve. I walked into his office and told him I wanted to read everything he had about the Jena Five. The next stop was the courthouse where I asked for the trial transcripts. I read those until my eyes crossed. I spent the night with Daddy and Kathy, not telling them why I was in Jena. I told them I had a free day, so I decided to drive down and see them.

The next day, I went and spoke to the parents of all the boys. I found out when the noose incident happened, the school board said the nooses were hung as a prank directed at white members of the school rodeo team. Ms. Felecia told me the school's investigating committee stated that "the three young teens who hung the nooses had no knowledge what they symbolized and were not familiar with the terrible legacy of lynchings of countless blacks in American history."

I just stared at her. Every person who lived in Louisiana or anywhere in the South, for that matter, knew what a lynching was. The names of the three boys who hung the nooses were never released. They received three days of in-school suspension. Ms. Felecia also told me that the Jena Five had an all-white jury. She said during the trial, the school superintendent stated publicly that "adolescents play pranks. I don't think it was a threat against anybody."

I could not believe what I was hearing. I told her I followed the trial on the news when it happened but had never heard any of what she was telling me. She said none of it came out in the trial. The FBI classified the hanging of the nooses as a hate crime, but there was no state or federal statute to charge juveniles. I found out the Southern Poverty Law Center tried to bring in their own attorneys for the boys, but the judge said the boys already had attorneys and it was too late for them to change.

Ms. Felicia told me that about a month after Willie went to prison, he tied two bedsheets together, hung them from a pipe in his cell, and jumped. The sheets came untied, and he fell to the floor. After that, he was on suicide watch for several months. I thanked her for her time, walked out to my car, got in, and drove back to Baton Rouge.

When I returned, I sat down and typed up a five-part series on the Jena Five; then I sent it to the editor of the Baton Rouge *Advocate* and the LSU newspaper who both agreed to publish it.

The backlash was instant. I received hate calls and threats and was called a nigger lover so many times that I lost count. It didn't weaken my resolve. Daddy found out about it, and one weekend when I was home, he gave me a .22 Ruger and took me target shooting. I took the gun with me everywhere I went.

I decided to accept the internship with the SPLC. I figured getting out of Louisiana for a couple of months would be a good thing. I called Mr. Dees to give him the news, and two weeks after I finished my sophomore year, I packed my bags and headed to Atlanta.

Chapter Forty

I decided to drive because I wanted to have my car with me to do some weekend exploring. The Dees lived in Roswell, Georgia, which was located right outside the city of Atlanta. They had a beautiful brick home with ivy climbing up the sides. Mrs. Dees was extremely nice and insisted I call her Susan. She took me to my room and told me to unpack and freshen up. Dinner would be served in thirty minutes. The room I was staying in was much bigger than my bedroom at the apartment. There were fresh flowers in a vase on the bedside table. The carpet was brown and lush. I sat on the bed. It felt comfortable. I washed my face and hands, brushed my hair, and made my way to the dining room.

"I hope you like Cornish game hens," Susan said.

I didn't tell her I had never tasted one.

"That sounds great! Thank you."

About that time, Mr. Dees walked in the front door, came over, and shook my hand.

"Christie! Welcome to Atlanta."

I thanked him for both the internship and a place to stay. Susan brought the food out, and it all looked and smelled wonderful. The game hen tasted like chicken to me. After we ate and had coffee and cake, Mr. Dees started talking about Willie Purvis. He asked me how he was doing. I told him about my visit with him at Angola. I told him I felt Willie had given up. We talked about Willie's trial, and I filled him in on some of the things Felicia had shared with me that I didn't put in the series. Mr. Dees said he hadn't wanted to tell me until I arrived, but he had filed an appeal on Willie's behalf. He was trying to have his conviction overturned. He said Willie should have never been tried as an adult, and there was no evidence that he had been the ringleader. He asked me to keep it to myself until we heard something from Louisiana. He didn't call Felicia because he didn't want to get her hopes up. I promised I wouldn't say a word. I started my internship the next day.

I loved working at the law center. I was finally surrounded by people who had the same thoughts and ideals I had. They all wanted to do whatever they could to bring about positive change in civil rights. This didn't just include the rights of black people but also women's rights. More women were working outside the home than ever before, and they were being pigeonholed into secretarial positions because the men in charge didn't believe a woman could do just as good a job as a man.

The employees at the center would give me a subject and ask me to write an editorial. Sometimes, they would give me several pages and I would research the rest; and sometimes, they would just give me a paragraph and I would start from scratch. I loved the job and felt like what I was doing could make a real difference in people's lives. My editorials were being published in big-name newspapers like the *New York Times* and the *San Francisco Chronicle*. Amy was extremely jealous. Several of her articles had been published in Louisiana newspapers but none out of state. She was interning at the *Advocate* in Baton Rouge. She said all she did was make coffee, but she was making contacts as well.

While I was in Atlanta, I enjoyed everything the city had to offer. I went to a couple of bars with some of the people from the center, and they couldn't believe I was only nineteen years old. Several of the guys asked me out, but I just wasn't interested. I had let Greg go, but I still wanted the type of relationship we had; and so far, no one had given me that tingly feeling. Sometimes, I wished for a steady boyfriend to hang out with, but it wasn't a priority. I was too busy enjoying my life. The first week of August rolled around, and my internship was over. Mr. Dees invited me back the next summer, but I told him I was shooting for an internship with a publisher in New York City. He wrote me a glowing recommendation letter. I had kept a portfolio of all my published articles and editorials to mimeograph and send in with my internship applications the next year. The staff gave me a going-away party, and I had way too much to drink, but it was fun. I had so much respect for the people I met while working at the center. They were true trailblazers. The day after the party, I packed my car and headed back to Louisiana.

Chapter Forty-One

Junior year began in earnest, and by the second week, I understood why everyone said it was the toughest year. I was taking six classes so I could graduate a semester early. All I did was study and write papers. Amy and I were rooming together again but had moved into a nicer apartment. Daddy was helping offset some of the cost, and I had every dollar I had made since I started working for Dr. Roose. Daddy told me to save that money for New York. Amy had decided she wanted to work at the *New York Times*, so we were going to move to the city together. She was also taking extra classes so we could finish college together.

Two weeks before my twentieth birthday, Amy convinced me to take a break and go with her to a house party on campus. There was a guy she liked who was supposed to be there, and she didn't want to go by herself. When we arrived, she made a beeline for her "next victim" as she called him, and I walked over to the keg and asked for a cup of beer. One thing I would not miss about college was beer from a keg. I went and sat down on a couch in the corner of the room and tried to ignore the couple next to me with their tongues stuck down each other's throats. I was about to go find Amy and tell her I was heading home when a tall, dark-haired guy walked up and said hi. I knew he was prelaw because he had been in my Civil Rights Law class the year before, but I couldn't remember his name.

"Mike."

"Excuse me?"

"My name. It's Mike."

"I knew that."

"No, you didn't." We both laughed.

He pulled up a lawn chair and sat down.

"So I heard you interned at the Southern Poverty Law Center last summer."

"I did."

"Is Morris Dees as brilliant as everyone says?"

"Yes, he is, but he's also really nice."

"Double threat."

We started talking about my internship, and he brought up the series I wrote about the Jena Five. He said he thought it was great. He was originally from Michigan, but his dad and his granddad had both gone to LSU law school, so there had never been any discussion about him going anywhere else. His grandfather had passed away four years earlier, and his dad owned a company in Dallas that made liquid CO_2.

Mike wanted to be a prosecutor. He said he would like to practice in New York or Boston where law and politics weren't as incestuous as they were in the South. I told him about my plan to move to New York City and work at a publishing house while working on my first novel. After a couple of hours, I told him I needed to go home. He asked for my number, and I gave it to him. He was the most interesting guy I had talked to in a long time, not to mention he was extremely cute. I said goodbye and started looking for Amy.

I couldn't find her anywhere, so I decided to walk back to our apartment by myself. I felt safe knowing I had my Ruger in my purse. I kept my hand on it as I walked across campus. Amy wasn't at the apartment when I got home, so I assumed she got lucky. I washed my face and went to bed.

A loud pounding on the front door woke me around three thirty. Someone was keening, and I couldn't make out what they were saying. I jumped up, grabbed my robe, and went to the door. I looked through the peephole and saw Amy. She was covered in blood. The sound she was making didn't sound human. I quickly opened the door, and she fell into my arms. Her face was swollen and puffy, and her clothes were ripped. I pulled her inside and closed the door. She was still making that noise, and I couldn't get her to stop.

I went in the kitchen, poured a shot of whiskey in a glass, and took it back to her.

"Amy, drink this. AMY, now! Drink it."

She took the glass and threw her head back, swallowing all of it in one gulp.

"Amy, what happened? Honey, talk to me. Who did this? Amy, Amy, please talk to me."

Her eyes finally focused on me. "Remember the guy I went to the party to see?"

"Yes."

"We had a couple of beers at the party; then he asked me to come back to his apartment for a real drink. We were talking and laughing all the way to his place, and when we got inside, he slammed the door shut and locked three dead bolts. He started calling me names, bitch, whore, cockteaser."

She started crying uncontrollably, so I went and got another shot and gave it to her. She calmed down enough to go on with the story.

"I told him to unlock the door that I was ready to leave."

"He grabbed me by the neck and pushed me up against the wall. He told me I wasn't going anywhere. He said he had plans for me. He backhanded me across the face, splitting my lip. Then he grabbed the front of my shirt and ripped it all the way down. Then he, he."

She began to shake. I sat beside her and put both arms around her, but I could not hold her still. She jumped up and ran to the bathroom. I could hear her vomiting. I went in the bathroom and wet a washcloth for her face. Her left eye was turning purple and was almost swollen shut; her lip was cut and swollen. She threw up until nothing but bile came out. I sat down beside her on the bathroom floor and began to wipe her forehead.

"Amy, we need to take you to the hospital. You need to be examined by a doctor."

"Nooo," she wailed. "No one can know about this ever. You have to promise me, please, Christie."

"Honey, he has probably done this before, and he will do it again. I can't imagine how scared you are right now or how you feel, but you must do this. You are a fighter. You don't take shit from anyone. Don't let this asshole take that away from you."

"What will they do to me at the hospital?"

"I'm not sure, but I read something in the *Times* about a specific kit they have that can help gather evidence to prove someone has been raped. I will stay with you the entire time, I promise."

"Okay. I don't want this to happen to anyone else."

I helped her up but wouldn't let her brush her teeth. I remembered from the article I read that you shouldn't shower, douche, or brush your teeth. I helped her put on a different shirt, and I put the torn shirt in a plastic Ziploc bag. I called the police from our apartment and asked them to meet us at the hospital. I drove us to the emergency room and helped Amy inside. I quietly told the woman sitting behind the desk what had happened. She made a call, and a few minutes later, a nurse came and took us back to an exam room. She said a forensic nurse would have to conduct the rape kit, but she was on her way. We sat on the table, and I held Amy as she sobbed and shook.

"Amy, what was the guy's name?"

"Eric. Eric Prest."

There was a knock on the door, and I said, "Come in." It was two Baton Rouge police officers. They both looked extremely uncomfortable. They told Amy they needed to ask her some questions. They told me to wait outside, but Amy told them she wanted me to stay. They asked her the name of the perpetrator. She told them, and they looked at each other.

"Are you sure it was Eric Prest?"

"Yes."

They looked at each other again.

"What?" I asked.

One of the police officers told us Eric's dad was the attorney general of Louisiana. I told them I didn't give a good goddamn if he was the president's son. He had beaten and raped my friend, and I wanted his ass in jail. They asked me to calm down. At this point, I was shaking as much as Amy, but mine was from anger. They began to question Amy. They didn't come out and say it, but they made it very clear that there was nothing they could do. She had went willingly to his apartment, and if they asked him, he would tell them it was just rough sex. There was no proof she had been raped. I told them we were waiting on the nurse to conduct a rape kit. The fat officer, who I had nicknamed Porky in my head, said that would only prove they had sex, not that she had been raped.

I screamed at them both. "Are you fucking blind? Look at her face. You do not get that from rough sex. He assaulted her. And because his daddy is a big shot and the two of you have no balls, you are trying to make this out to be her fault. She was raped!"

They threatened to take me to jail if I didn't stop yelling. I told them I would sleep better at night knowing the two of them were in charge. Then I told them to get the fuck out. They left.

Amy had stopped crying and was sitting on the exam table, staring straight ahead. I knew she was in shock. There was another knock on the door, and a nurse came in. She told us she had spoken to the police, and they told her they believed it was rough sex that got out of hand.

The nurse asked Amy if she still wanted her to perform the rape kit. Amy said she just wanted to go home and take a shower. The nurse and I looked at each other. She wrote Amy a prescription for pain medication and told her to go to her doctor in three months to make sure she didn't have an STD. Amy nodded her head, and I helped her out to the car and took her home. She stood in the shower for two hours screaming at the top of her lungs. I sat outside with my head leaning against the door until she stopped.

Chapter Forty-Two

Amy's physical wounds healed, but emotionally, she was shattered. She refused to leave the apartment, and sometimes, she didn't shower or eat for days. She was going through a bottle of Jack Daniel's a week, and I finally told her I wasn't going to buy the whiskey for her anymore. I thought that would end her drinking, but she just called the liquor store and arranged for them to deliver it to her. She received an F in all her classes and lost her job at the campus newspaper. I had no idea how to help her. Fall semester ended, and I was planning on going back to Jena for the holidays, but I was afraid to leave her alone. I finally called her parents and told them what happened. They said they would come immediately to pick her up. I knew I had to tell her. I walked into her room, and the smell made me gag. It smelled like stale sweat and vomit.

"Amy, your parents are on their way."

She looked at me through bleary, bloodshot eyes. "What? Why?"

"I called them and told them what happened. You can't go on like this."

"Who the fuck do you think you are? I know what you think of me. You think I deserved it because I slept around. Well, we can't all have one love our entire lives."

I sat down on the side of her bed. She smelled awful.

"Amy, of course, I don't think you deserved it. No one deserves that. You haven't done any more than any other college student; you just mistakenly picked a psychopath. Go home, heal, and finish your education. You will always have a room in New York with me."

She started crying, reached over, and hugged me tight. "I'm sorry. I'm not the same person, Christie. He took everything from me. My dreams, my plans, my life!"

"Only if you let him. You cannot let him win, Amy. Let's get you in the shower and clean this place up before your parents get here." I helped her to the shower. I threw out all the empty liquor bottles and washed the sheets and all her clothes. I sprayed her room with Lysol and lit a candle. When I was finished, it still smelled a little, but it was 100 percent better. Amy came out dressed with her hair in a towel.

"I want to thank you."

I held up my hand. "Don't. It's not necessary. It's what best friends do. You would have done the same thing for me."

She sat cross-legged on her bed and said, "So tell me about this Mike guy."

I laughed. There was still some Amy in there. "How did you know?"

"I heard you guys talking on the phone. I heard you say his name, and I heard you laughing. I've never heard you laugh that much with a guy. You sounded happy."

"He's a great guy, but it's still very new. He is prelaw. He wants to put bad guys in jail."

"Sounds like a match made in heaven. I'm happy for you."

Someone knocked on the door.

I went and opened the door for Amy's parents. Amy walked out of her bedroom. She saw her parents and began to cry. She rushed into their arms, and they held her for a long time. Her mom helped her pack while her dad talked to me. He wanted to know exactly what happened. So I told him. I could see his jaw working.

"And just exactly where can I find this Eric Prest?"

"I'm not sure. He dropped out of school. I haven't seen him."

Amy and her mother walked out of her bedroom with a couple of suitcases. Amy refused to pack up the rest of her things because she was determined she was coming back for the winter semester. I walked them out to the car. Amy hugged me and said, "Thank you. I love you." I told her she was welcome, and I loved her too. I watched their car until it was out of sight. I went back upstairs, packed my bag, and headed to Jena.

It was a great holiday. Kathy's daughters came, and I really liked them both. My dad and Kathy were wonderful together and completely in love with each other. It was nice to see Daddy so happy. Mike called several times. He was in Dallas with this dad and stepmom. His mother had died when he was eleven, so his stepmom basically raised him. Daddy answered the phone once when he called, and when I hung up, he said, "Is he a Yankee?" We both laughed, and he told me how happy he was for me.

Two weeks later, I headed back to Baton Rouge.

Chapter Forty-Three

The winter semester began, and I was taking eighteen credit hours and writing for the Baton Rouge *Advocate*. The article I wrote about the indifference the police showed to rape victims was on the front page. I called for tougher laws for perpetrators. The story was picked up by a newspaper in Houston; then the *New York Times* wrote an exposé about "America's Dirty Secret" and used excerpts from my article in the story. It was a big deal, and Mike took me out to celebrate. We had been dating for several months, and we were getting to the point in our relationship to move to the next step. I was ready.

Mike took me to a beautiful restaurant, and when the evening was almost over, I asked him if he wanted to spend the night at my apartment. He said he would like that very much. He stayed the entire weekend.

Mike was in his first year of law school, so every spare moment he had was spent studying. I was busy as well, but we saw each other as much as we could and made a point to do something together on at least one day each weekend.

One night, we were at a bar with some of Mike's friends and their girlfriends. I was having a great time, and then I looked up and saw Eric. Amy had transferred to LSU in Shreveport, and I dipped into my savings so I could have the apartment to myself. She was still suffering from extreme anxiety. When I saw Eric, my body began to shake, and I felt the anger stir inside of me. I reached in my purse and felt my gun. I wanted to take it out and blow his head off, but he wasn't worth going to prison for.

Mike asked me what was wrong, and I told him. He looked over at Eric and then said something to his two friends. There was a roaring sound in my ears, and I didn't hear what he said. He told me he would be right back.

Mike and two of his friends walked over to Eric. Mike leaned in and said something in his ear. Eric's lip curled up, and he got off the barstool and pushed Mike. Mike punched him in the face, then threw him on the floor, and began to pound him in the face. Mike's friends held everyone back. Mike didn't stop until the bartender threatened to call the police. Mike gave him one final kick and walked back to our table.

"We need to go."

I grabbed my purse, and we walked out. On the way back to my apartment, I put my hand on his arm and thanked him. He smiled at me and reached for my hand. I could see blood on his knuckles, and they were turning blue. When we got back to my place, I cleaned his hand and gave him a bag of ice to hold on his knuckles. I called Amy and told her what happened. She wanted to speak to Mike. He told her he was happy to do it. I could hear Amy talking and crying. They talked for a few more minutes and then hung up.

"I think she likes me." He grinned.

"I told him it was time for bed."

I fell asleep with Mike's arms around me.

Chapter Forty-Four

My junior year of college ended, and I didn't get the internship at Warner Books, so I went back to Atlanta to work for the law center. I was able to convince Mr. Dees to give Mike an internship as well so we could be together all summer. I was excited to be returning to Atlanta, but I didn't feel the work I did at the center was going to help me obtain a job with a publishing house in New York.

Mike and I arrived in Atlanta in early June. I would be staying with the Dee's again, and Mike was going to rent a room in a house with a group of guys from the center. We jumped in with both feet when we arrived and didn't complain about the fourteen-hour days. Usually, a bunch of us went to the bars in Buckhead after work. None of us could afford more than one drink, so someone would sneak in a flask and use the contents to replenish our drinks. Mike and I grew closer and closer though it was hard to find any time to be alone. I would be graduating in December, and Mike still had two years of law school left, so we didn't talk much about the future.

I spoke to Amy every other week or so. She was dating a friend of her brother who was also a marine. He lived in California, and things were serious enough between them that he asked her to move out there and live with him. She wanted to finish college first; she only had one more year. He told her he would wait. I was happy for her. Daddy called and told me Scout had passed away. He choked up when he told me. I was sad for him and sad Scout died, but she had ceased being my dog a long time ago.

In the middle of July, right before Mike and I went back to Baton Rouge, Mr. Dees called me into his office. He was pacing the floor, which was nothing new. He was always moving and gesturing wildly, especially if he was excited.

"Christie, I have some great news. The state of Louisiana threw out Willie's conviction. They said his trial wasn't legal because he was tried as an adult when his past crimes didn't warrant it. He is going to be released on Saturday."

I yelled, ran over, and hugged Mr. Dees. We were both jumping up and down.

"I haven't called Willie's mother. I know you two have a history. I thought you might want to be the one to give her the news."

I thanked him and went into the small conference room we used for meetings. I closed the door and dialed the number. Felicia was living in Ernestine's house, and I knew the telephone number by heart. She answered after the third ring.

"Hello?"

"Felicia, this is Christie. Are you sitting down?"

I gave her the news, and at first, she didn't believe me. I explained that Mr. Dees had written the appeal, but we hadn't told her because we didn't want to get her hopes up. I told her it was true. Willie was going to be released Saturday morning.

"I don't know how to thank you."

"It wasn't me. Mr. Dees did all the work."

"Yes, but those stories you wrote made him interested in Willie's case. He never would have known otherwise."

I told her I never believed Willie was the ringleader, and I thought there had been a serous miscarriage of justice. I just wanted other people to know as well. I told her I had to go but to please tell Willie I said hello. She said she would.

"Christie?"

"Yes?"

"Mama would have been so proud of you."

I choked out a thank-you and hung up. I went to tell Mike the good news. Three weeks later, we headed back to LSU.

Chapter Forty-Five

The fall semester began, and I was taking twenty-one credits so I could graduate in December. Everyone thought I was crazy. I had to get special permission from the registrar to take that many classes. I gave up my job at the newspaper. I knew there was no way I could keep up with my classes and work. Mike started his second year of law school. We knew our time was coming to an end, but we never talked about it.

Mr. Dees knew someone who knew someone else who was able to set up an interview for me with Random House. I flew to New York the last week of October to interview for the job. New York City was everything I dreamed it would be. I could understand why people said it was "the city that never sleeps." I could hear people outside my hotel room all hours of the day and night. I was interviewing for a proofreader position, which was fine with me. I would get paid to correct other people's work all day, which meant I would be reading all day. I was thrilled. I only spent two days and one night in the city, but I knew it was where I wanted to be.

Random House called me the third week of November and told me I had the job. I was due to start on January 15. I called Daddy first, and he and Kathy were so happy for me. That night, I told Mike, and he told me how happy he was and how proud he was of me.

"I have some news of my own," he said.

"Really, what is it?"

"Last year, I applied to Columbia Law School in New York. I received an acceptance letter last week."

I squealed. “Why didn’t you tell me?”

“Because I wanted to make sure you got the job at Random House first.”

We looked at each other as we both realized what this meant. Mike was going to New York just so he could be with me. It was a huge step. I never thought of myself as the marrying type, but with Mike, that all seemed possible. The life I had dreamed of since I was six years old was about to begin.

“I love you, Christie.”

“I love you too.”

About the Author

Ms. Collins was born and raised in the Deep South where sweet tea, seafood gumbo, and "bless your heart" were commonplace. Ms. Collins was recently published in Chicken Soup for the Soul: My Crazy Family. She began writing short stories when she was six years old, and two years ago, she decided to try her hand at writing a full-time. Before taking time off to write, she was the director of several nonprofit agencies, including United Way and Habitat for Humanity. She lives in the upper Midwest with her husband, Mike, and their Coondog, Lincoln. Ms. Collins has a bachelor's degree in criminal justice administration and a master's degree in organizational leadership both from Concordia University Ann Arbor. Ms. Collins is currently working on a true crime account of a murder that occurred in mid-Michigan in 1977 and was closed thirty years later without a conviction. Sunshine through the Rain is her first novel.

CPSIA information can be obtained
at www.ICGtesting.com
Printed in the USA
FFHW020828070119
50063444-54884FF